HOME FIRES

Dixie DuBois

A KISMET® Romance

METEOR PUBLISHING CORPORATION
Bensalem, Pennsylvania

This book is dedicated to Frankie Grovenburg Broussard and Janet Hains Lewis.

DIXIE DuBOIS

Dixie Lewis Gaspard has been a storyteller since the age of nine. Her love of reading romances led her to begin writing them ten years ago. Married to her high school sweetheart for twenty-five years, she has two children and is awaiting the birth of her first grandchild.

Vickie Hillman DuBois grew up in the piney woods of Mississippi reading Faulkner, Dickens, and Twain. Then she discovered Rosemary Rogers and Kathleen Woodiwiss. Inspired, she began writing romances. She found her own romantic hero 19 years ago and they have two teenaged sons.

ONE

Oh no! It can't be him—it can't be!

Leara James Lockwood stood frozen in the main aisle of Ferguson's Market, gripping the handle of her shopping cart like a lifeline. She stared at the dark-haired man studying the selection of toothpastes in the health and beauty aids aisle.

She took in every feature in a glance—those thick-lashed, sherry brown eyes, the straight brows, that aquiline nose, those sensual lips—and her heart confirmed the worst.

It was him.

But he wasn't the same boyishly handsome college sophomore that she remembered. Not quite. He was older, of course. She was twenty-eight, so he must be thirty now. And he was even more handsome than the mental picture she'd carried with her all these years.

He had changed. The boyishness was gone. In its place, he wore an air of self-assurance with the same ease with which he wore his perfectly tailored wool-blend suit. The silver-gray suit, white shirt, and navy tie set off his light tan and short dark hair.

7

Leara's heart beat wildly as he turned and those brown eyes met hers.

Don't let him recognize me!

Turning away quickly, Leara ducked around the end of the next aisle and accidentally rammed her cart into a pyramid display of canned peas. She cringed as several cans smacked the floor, making only slightly less noise than a sonic boom, then rolled away in every direction.

Maybe he wouldn't notice the racket, she thought frantically as she sank to her knees to retrieve the fallen cans. Maybe he was already on his way to the checkout.

Maybe, she wouldn't have to face him!

Or maybe she would! Leara groaned inwardly as she looked up after grabbing the last stray can. The long legs before her belonged to Garreth Conroe—the man she'd run out on ten years ago.

"I don't believe it!" said a familiar masculine voice.

Garreth's large hand grasped hers. He pulled her erect, and she found herself staring up into his warm brown eyes.

"Leara?"

She felt her cheeks flush as those eyes made a sweeping appraisal of her, and she realized how she must look. Her faded jeans hugged her hips and thighs, and the too-small orange T-shirt strained over her breasts.

When she had dug these clothes out of the chest in her old room, she'd thought that they'd be perfect for housecleaning. She was suddenly aware that they gave off a musty odor from being packed away for so long. And, Lord, her hair was a mess! She'd tied a frayed red bandana over her unruly copper-colored curls to keep off the worst of the dust. Leara ran her fingers through the damp locks on her forehead and prayed fervently that at least there weren't any smudges on her face.

"Leara! It is you!"

Garreth's arms engulfed her. She found herself crushed to his broad chest. His cologne gave off a faint, totally intoxicating musk scent. She thought vaguely that his shoulders were much wider than she remembered. Then his lips were on hers and the sensations that she had tried to forget for ten years flooded through her. The familiar electric tingling rushed from her spinning head clear to her toes, threatening to make her knees buckle. She was grateful that he still held her close when the kiss ended.

"Hello, Garreth." With her body caught in his enthusiastic embrace, her words came out garbled. It felt right to be in his arms, his heart beating beneath her palm. She wanted to stay nestled there. She felt a little lost when he finally released her.

"Leara, I can't believe it's you. What are you doing in Columbus? Have you moved back?" His eyes swept her again, and he squeezed her arms as if to assure himself that she was real.

Her joy at the welcoming expression on his face was so intense that she tore her eyes from him before he could see it. *Easy, girl. He's just happy to see an old friend.*

And they had been friends. Very close friends.

"My . . . uh . . . father died last month and left Gram's house to me. I came down to sort through the things in the house and get it ready for sale."

She still couldn't believe he was here. The last she'd heard, Garreth had become a successful architect and was living in Chicago.

Over time, the wild feelings left over from their youthful romance had faded to the special poignancy that she imagined most people must feel when they thought of their first love. She'd been certain she'd never see him again.

But if she were honest with herself, she'd admit that some part of her had always hoped . . .

Now, as she looked up into his eyes, all those emotions came rushing back. Despite the odds, Garreth was here. With her. In this town, which she'd begged him to help her escape from all those years ago. Suddenly, face to face with him again, that last night long ago sprang vividly into her mind. . . .

Leara had known it was a mistake to meet Garreth. She'd reluctantly agreed because she couldn't bear to leave town without seeing him again. She got into his car at the corner down from Gram's house, so her father wouldn't see her.

Garreth stared straight ahead in stony silence until she closed the car door, then he shifted the engine into gear. Before she realized where he was going, the car was barreling along the road to Tarzan's Lake, the speed mirroring Garreth's inner turmoil. He braked to a stop where the road ended by the railroad tracks, turned, and pulled her into his arms. Kissing her desperately, he pulled her close, fitting his body to hers.

Leara quaked inside from the need that instantly pounded through her. She loved him. Now. Tomorrow. Forever. She knew he felt the same. Why couldn't he just give in to these beautiful feelings, to the love that could solve everything?

She wound her arms around his neck, and he deepened the kiss, trying to bind her to him. When he broke away, he was panting.

"Leara, you can't marry Quint!" he said against her neck. "He's no good. You don't love him; I know you don't!"

"So, you'll marry me?" she asked. Garreth's hands

closed around her arms as he pulled back from her. His face was ravaged, but he shook his head.

"Then I don't care!" Leara shouted to him. She pushed against his arms, but he held her firmly. "I can't stand it here anymore!"

She drew in a deep breath and willed herself to calm down. "Look," she said when she'd regained some control, "I don't have any money of my own. I don't even have a life of my own since Gram died and Dad staged his military takeover. He's got my life all mapped out. He's already enrolled me in secretarial school, and he expects me to continue to live at home under his stupid rules and regulations. He's even got a job lined up for me with Johnson's Insurance for when I've finished! I can't stand it! I'm eighteen years old now and I won't do it! I'd rather marry you, you know that! But I can't wait around for two more years while you finish college. I wouldn't survive it!" Hot tears drenched her cheeks. Garreth seemed not to see.

"All right, Leara." Garreth released her. She shivered at the coldness in his expression, at the icy tone of his voice. "You've made your choice."

And she had, a frantic eighteen-year-old's choice. It had been the last time she'd seen him, felt his arms around her. There had been no soft good-bye, no farewell kiss that night. Only bitterness. She hadn't been able to force Garreth to marry her to help her escape her father's domination, so she'd married Quint Lockwood instead. And it had been the mistake that Garreth had predicted.

Now here he was—smiling at her—as though the pain had never happened.

Leara composed herself and looked up at Garreth. She searched his eyes; in the past his emotions had always been clearly revealed in them. There was warmth in the reddish brown depths. And joy. But wasn't it just the joy of a man discovering a friend from years past?

Well, that was okay. After the way she'd left him for another man, she didn't deserve anything. At least he was happy to see her.

"You've changed, Garreth," Leara told him.

"You haven't. You still look eighteen." He smiled at her and she felt like that schoolgirl again.

"I guess the wardrobe doesn't help." She looked ruefully at her old jeans and the dirty deck shoes on her feet.

"I don't know. I think the outfit is sexy," he teased. His eyes lingered on her breasts outlined by the snug T-shirt, and she felt another blush creep up her neck to her cheeks.

Why was she shocked by his flirting? It was ten years later, but this was still Garreth. The Garreth who had always teased a smile out of her. The Garreth who had known her every secret, held her when she cried, looked at her with the eyes of a man, who'd been the first . . .

The blush deepened as other vivid memories surged through her in a warm flood.

"What about you?" she asked quickly, trying to hide her embarrassment. "What brings you back to the old neighborhood?"

"We're living here now. Don't look so surprised. I started out in Chicago instead of here in Columbus only because no kid fresh out of college could get a job designing a doghouse in this town before he'd proven himself. And because . . . well, I guess I was looking for something . . . a faster pace, maybe. This town may be the mecca of modern architecture, but its still a Midwest town surrounded by cornfields."

"You're back? For good?" Leara asked. *Easy, girl,*

easy. What does it matter if he's back? Even if he is, you aren't.

"Yes. I guess I took the boy out of the cornfields, but I couldn't take the cornfields out of the boy. I still have a share of the firm in Chicago, but I find I'd rather design homes than glass towers. Right now, I'm working on some housing renewal projects with a local developer. We're renovating homes in some older sections of town, modernizing the interiors, adding more bathrooms and closet space. We're offering the units at affordable prices, mostly to young families. It's great to help people realize their dreams of owning their own home. Otherwise, they might have to wait years."

He chuckled ruefully. "That came out sounding self-important. I guess I wanted you to think I'm doing something useful with my life. Remember all the times we talked about how we were going to set the world on fire?"

"Sure." But, as Leara thought about it, she really couldn't remember talking about her dreams in those days. She couldn't remember having any. She'd been too much in love to think beyond Garreth. She did remember Garreth talking about all the great things he wanted to do while she listened in adoration.

Garreth smiled slowly. Looking into his incredibly sexy eyes, she understood why she hadn't thought beyond Garreth.

Leara returned his smile. The silence lengthened. They had run out of meaningless things to say. All the unspoken thoughts and memories were almost tangible between them, charging the air. Then Garreth took her hand and that familiar bolt of electricity shot through her.

A high-pitched voice broke the silence. "Daddy! Daddy, aren't you ever coming?"

A tiny blond girl darted under the chain at an empty

checkout stand and wrapped herself around Garreth's leg. His big hand ruffled her curls as she looked up at him. "C'mon, Daddy! I thought you were just getting me some toothpaste. We've been waiting in the car forever—and it's hot!"

Noticing Leara for the first time, she turned large brown eyes—the exact color of her father's—toward the strange woman. She gave Leara a quick assessing glance, then said brightly, "Hi. Who're you?"

Leara came abruptly back to earth. "We're living here," Garreth had said. "We've been waiting," the child had said. She looked at the girl, the daughter he shared with his wife.

Leara squatted down to eye level with the little girl, glad to avoid Garreth's eyes, "Just an old friend of your daddy's," she said, and imitated the child's lilting tone as she asked, "Who are you?"

"Oh, I'm Jenny." The long-lashed brown eyes took stock a second time. "Do you have a little girl?"

The question came out of nowhere, catching Leara completely off guard, but the girl's smile was more timid now face to face, and Leara instinctively set about putting the child at ease. "No, I sure don't." Leara shoved aside the momentary stab of regret. "But if I did, I'd hope she'd be as pretty as you."

Jenny's grin seemed to indicate her approval of the compliment and of the speaker, for she turned to Garreth and asked, "Daddy, can the lady come have supper with us? I bet she likes pizza, too."

Panic filled Leara's mind with excuses. She couldn't. She was just regaining her balance after the divorce from Quint. She was putting the past behind her, finally. To see Garreth with his wife and child—laughing, happy—she wouldn't be able to bear it.

Garreth didn't notice her discomfort, because he told his daughter, "Sure, Jen. How about it, Leara?" His smile was warm and inviting. "The three of us were just going to Antonio's for takeout."

"Oh, no. I don't think so . . . not tonight." She couldn't look at him.

If she had, she'd have seen his disappointment.

"Well, how about lunch tomorrow? Just to talk over old times?"

That was worse. She wanted to bury old times. Forget them completely. The feeling of panic swept over her again.

"Maybe another day, Garreth," she lied. "I'm kind of busy now. The house, you know." *Keep it light, Leara*, she chided herself. *Besides, he's only being polite.*

"I'll hold you to it. C'mon, Jenny, say good-bye."

The little golden child waved to Leara as she followed her father to the checkout.

Leara turned away, suddenly aware that she still held a can of peas.

This is a mistake, Garreth said to himself as he parked his car in front of the white frame house on Oak Street. He'd come here so often when he was younger. Sitting here like this, he had a feeling of déjà vu. He half expected to see a gray-haired woman appear at the screened door and invite him inside.

But tonight is very different, Garreth reminded himself. Leara wasn't waiting for him to pick her up for a date. She was married to someone else. And she hadn't seemed thrilled by his casual invitation for lunch.

So, why the hell was he here?

Because, after all these years apart, he hadn't forgotten her. Those five minutes in Ferguson's Market just weren't enough. That kiss, the feel of her in his arms had brought those memories firmly into the present.

Even though she might not feel the same way about him, he had to see her again. Just once more.

He'd come to extend a dinner invitation to her—and to her husband.

He had never liked Quint Lockwood. They were the same age, though Quint had been in Leara's class in high school. Lockwood was a braggart and a bully back then, and Garreth had never been able to forget that Leara had dated Quint first. Maybe, it had been a premonition that she'd ultimately choose him.

Come off it, Conroe! She didn't choose Lockwood. You pushed her straight into his arms!

Maybe Quint has changed over the years. A woman like Leara was certainly reason enough to change. She had seemed happy when he had seen her in Ferguson's Market. Maybe her marriage to Quint had been the right thing for her after all. Maybe she was happy.

Happy. Content. With Quint.

Could he stand seeing them together? Maybe this dinner invitation wasn't such a good idea.

No, damn it! If he wanted to see her again, it would have to be with Quint. He would assure himself she was as happy as she had seemed. Maybe then he could forget her.

As Garreth climbed the wooden steps, he noticed that the lawn had been cut recently. Its fragrance permeated the early evening air, carrying him back to summer nights long ago. How many summer nights had he come to pick her up? And Leara was always eagerly waiting—but not tonight. Tonight, he'd find her with her husband.

Light spilled through the screened door as Garreth took a deep breath and raised his hand to knock. The movement was arrested by the sight of Leara inside, seated cross-legged in the middle of the hardwood floor. She was surrounded by boxes. The light from the ceiling fixture turned her coppery hair almost golden. He couldn't see her face, hidden in the shadow of her curls. She was bent over the high school yearbook in her lap.

She looked so tiny as she slowly turned the pages, her hand running in a caress down each. She closed the book and sat very still for a long moment, then opened it again to the inside front cover. Garreth felt his heart constrict as he watched her gently trace the words written there.

Garreth remembered those words; he'd written them the day after Leara's senior prom—the day after they'd made love for the first time:

To my Cinderella,
You didn't need a fairy godmother last night. No princess could have been more beautiful. And you are even more beautiful to me now. When we left the · ball at midnight, the magic had just begun. Then you lost your slipper. But, I'm not sorry, because you gave it to me . . .

TWO

Leara smiled as she read the rest of the words:

Now, you're truly my princess.
One day soon I'll carry you off to my castle.
And we'll live Happily Ever After. Promise.

> *I'll love you always,*
> *Your Prince Charming*

The words vividly recalled for her the first time they'd made love.

Garreth had lowered her to the blanket, his youthful muscles rippling in the moonlight, his face in shadow, his eyes glowing with desire as they explored her body.

Leara felt no fear, only the consuming hunger to be part of him. As his warm fingers explored her and she savored the taste of his skin against her mouth, a pulsing ache began deep inside her. . . .

A sharp knocking only partially roused Leara from the vivid memory. She looked up. Garreth was standing in the shadows beyond the screen door, an apparition, as if her memory had become real. He wore snug jeans and a white cotton shirt, the long sleeves folded up to his elbows. It was a moment before Leara realized he was actually standing there; he wasn't part of her dream.

No! What was he doing here? And did he have to be here right now? Now—when the memory of that wonderful night together made her feel so open, so vulnerable!

"Hello, Leara." His voice was husky, almost as if he could read her thoughts, feel her emotions. Leara blushed.

"Garreth . . . come in." She stumbled to her feet, the forgotten yearbook falling to the floor with a thud. She swung the screened door wide. Garreth's presence seemed to fill the room as he stepped through the door.

A warm breeze from the open windows stirred the partially raised shades as Garreth touched the maple rocker of Leara's grandmother.

"I can almost see your grandmother sitting here, looking out the front window."

Leara nodded. From this spot Gram had kept track of the goings-on in the neighborhood. Watching life in the neighborhood had been her main recreation after she had been left idle by crippling rheumatoid arthritis.

Leara's lips curved into a nostalgic smile. "Remember how she would launch into hilarious character sketches of each person she saw? She'd invent comical situations and dialogue to fit the way the person dressed or walked and have the two of us laughing so hard that we couldn't catch our breath?"

"I admired that lady. She never let her illness get her down," Garreth said.

He knew that laughter and her grandmother's love had been healing for Leara. He remembered holding that teenaged Leara as she'd cried and told him how close she had been to her mother, who'd died from a sudden illness shortly after Leara had turned thirteen. And how her father, always remote, had retreated from her even further. Lost in his own pain, burying himself in his career as an Air Force officer, the man had refused to see how much his daughter needed him, or he just hadn't cared. For the next couple of years, Leara's home life had become a series of confrontations over her increasingly wild behavior. The confrontations had ended when the police had called Leara's father one day to come pick her up after she and her friends had gone joyriding—she hadn't known that the car one of the guys in the gang had ''borrowed'' was really stolen. Her father's answer had been to leave her to his mother's care.

Garreth remembered how close he'd felt to Leara as she'd shared her pain, and how much he'd empathized with her, for his own father had seldom been there for him when he'd needed him. But in the end, he'd let her down and let her marry Lockwood.

He started to ask where Quint was but thought better of it. He didn't really want to know. Moving to the box of memorabilia in the middle of the floor, he picked up the discarded yearbook and flipped through the pages to a photo of Leara in cap and gown. A musing smile briefly curved his mouth.

Leara stood nearby, unable to speak. The sight of Garreth's dark head bent over the remains of their past together stirred emotions that had been long buried. They threatened to overwhelm her. She felt too vulnerable for words, as if the box of keepsakes lying there was a window into her heart.

It had been ten years! How could she still feel the ache and disappointment so strongly? It didn't make sense.

When his brown eyes turned to her and seemed to

compare the Leara of today with the naive young girl in the photo, her knees nearly gave way.

Garreth's smile, when it came, broke through Leara's trance like sunlight through a cloud. "No. You haven't changed at all. Still my Cinderella."

For a moment she was stunned by his use of the old pet name, not sure why he had used it. She smiled back at him.

He sees us as just two old school chums reminiscing, she thought. *Okay. I can act the part.*

"What made you save all this stuff?" he asked.

"I found it in my old room. I . . . Dad never cleaned out my things. It's strange, but he seems to have just closed the door when I left."

She watched uneasily while Garreth shifted through the collection in the box. He cataloged each object. "A napkin from Bill and Marijo's wedding reception. You know, they should have put Kimmi's name on this, too. She was there, even if she didn't make an appearance for another five months." His deep chuckle filled the room. "That was a rush affair."

"No, the affair wasn't rushed—they dated for two years. Only the wedding was rushed," Leara said, grinning. "Marijo's mind was set on full-length wedding pictures. If they'd waited much longer, she'd have had to settle for head shots."

Leara looked up into his laughing brown eyes. Suddenly, it was easy being with him, reliving this part of her past.

"Besides, maternity wedding gowns aren't easy to find."

Garreth gave her a long, searching look before returning his attention to the box. He held out a menu they had "stolen" from Chez Edward, one of the classier restaurants in Columbus. He'd taken her there for her eighteenth birthday. It had been her first fancy dinner date. She remembered those same brown eyes gazing lovingly at her over their wine glasses—her first champagne—in the candlelight. Garreth had presented her with the menu, with the date of their special evening inscribed on the cover, as a keepsake of that night. She suspected he'd bought it.

"What's this?" Garreth had been digging in the box again. He held up something flat and crumbling.

"A rosebud from the corsage you gave me on prom night."

She could almost see Garreth in his black tux trying to pin the flowers on her strapless gown. Finally, he had grinned sheepishly and handed them to her.

The bold eyes that swept her now weren't those of that college boy of long ago. Leara reached out and took the fragile flower from him. As their fingers touched, her hand trembled. That night was so close, as though the years between had vanished.

Almost as if it had been preordained, the next thing he pulled from the box was their stone. About the size of an egg, the smooth gray rock was vaguely heart-shaped. Garreth had picked it up that night at Tarzan's Lake, on the ground near them. It had seemed like an omen that their love was intended by fate, and she had cherished it.

Leara looked up. Garreth's eyes were on her face, searching. Was the desire in them just a memory of that magical night? Was it only appreciation of an attractive female? Or was it spawned by the same magic chemistry that they had once shared? The thought awakened a surge of hunger that startled her with its intensity, and then a rush of panic.

It would be more than foolish to become involved with Garreth Conroe again. She was no longer that insecure teenager; the one who had fallen in love with his sureness of purpose, his calmly focused goals; the one who had been content to have him fit her into his life, his dreams. Then, her importance in his life had fallen somewhere between his design class and his ancient sedan and had been largely based on biology, she reminded herself. And, now, he was married.

As Leara watched Garreth's expression, his gaze moved to her lips. Anticipating the next move, her breath caught in her throat. Abruptly, she turned away. "You go ahead and reminisce," she called shakily over her shoulder as she headed for the kitchen. "I'm going to get us some iced tea."

Once she was safely out of Garreth's sight, she leaned against the kitchen counter. Her heart was thudding in her chest. It was almost as if she was afraid of him.

Leara thumped a fist on the counter. This was silly. She and Garreth were just old friends caught up in memories of first love; that was all. They had different lives now—separate lives that didn't include one another.

Anything else just wasn't possible.

Garreth caressed the heart-shaped stone in his hand. That night was so clear in his mind. Her skin, her smell, her heat. They had made love other times—wonderful times. But that night, the first time for both of them, had been magic. That kind of magic didn't just disappear because time and circumstance tore the people apart, did it? Was he just being sentimental? Maybe he had misread her expression when he'd come to the door. Perhaps, as Leara had been looking at her keepsakes of the two years that they had dated, the emotions in her eyes had just been empty echoes of something past.

When Leara returned with the tall glasses of tea, Garreth was sitting on the dusty sofa with the box of junk at his feet. Beside him, on the cushions, were the yearbook and a slender volume of *Sonnets from the Portuguese*.

Garreth had given her that book for her sixteenth birthday. They'd been dating only a few weeks. Her old-fashioned grandmother had been scandalized. Love poems for a sixteen-year-old? And what love poems!

He had awakened her to so much, that serious young man. Now, he sat across from her, his right ankle atop his left knee, one arm draped across the back of the sofa, casually sipping his tea. So cool. So self-assured. Like a photo in *Gentleman's Quarterly*. Somehow, not quite like her Garreth.

Her Garreth? That was all over long ago, she reminded herself firmly. He wasn't that person anymore. He was married, with a family. And part of a past she had put behind her.

So why is he here? Admit it, you should have asked that question when he appeared at the door. So why haven't you?

Because you realize you might not want to know the answer. Or, maybe, you already know it.

When she stared into his eyes, the look in their warm brown depths was blatantly provocative. She felt awareness of him throbbing through her in a primitive rhythm. She was alive to everything about him; the flash of his teeth when he smiled; the low, intimate timbre of his voice when he talked to her; the dark lights in his eyes as he gazed at her lips. Mesmerized, Leara felt as though she was falling into a trap that she had to avoid.

But she was helpless. Desire crackled between them like lightning. When Garreth reached across the gap and grasped her hand, the connection was complete and electric.

Her resolve not to fall into the trap was almost overpowered as the words of her favorite poem from the

sonnets spun round in her head: "Say thou dost love
me, love me, love me—toll the silver iterence!—only
minding, Dear, to love me also in silence with thy
soul."

Garreth softly stroked Leara's fingers, savoring the
texture of her skin, anxious to maintain this link with
her. These mementos scattered around them brought
back the past; clarified the feelings that he had shoved
down into some forgotten corner of his soul. He still
wanted her. He had never known a woman he wanted
more—not even the beautiful fashion model that he'd
been married to. And now he found Leara even more
beautiful, more appealing, than she had been as a
teenager.

Garreth's mind was a swirl of conflict. He wanted—
needed—to pull her into his arms; to feel her breath on
his skin; to make love to her; to make her his again,
though he'd found her again only a few hours ago.

But what about Quint? She had married Quint and
gone out of Garreth's life. He had no right to feel this
way.

Suddenly, Garreth released Leara's hand. She
blinked, hardly able to breathe. Her fingers still tingled
from the warm contact. She watched, dazed, as Garreth
leaned back and took a long sip of his tea. His eyes,
when he raised them again, were impenetrable. When
he spoke, his voice seemed to come from very far
away.

"So, where's Quint?"

Leara was stunned. Quint? She had forgotten about
Quint—so completely that, for a moment, Garreth's
question didn't make sense. Leara frowned. Why was
he asking about Quint?

"In Gary, I suppose. He sells cars at a dealership
near a day care center where I work." She was grateful
that her voice sounded calm, without the uneasiness

usually provoked by Quint's name. She hadn't talked to him in months. When she'd filed for divorce, he'd gone a little off the deep end. Leara had known for a long time that their marriage was over, but Quint wouldn't accept it. At the time Leara had decided that it was less a matter of Quint's undying love than his resentment that she had called it quits first.

Laura scanned Garreth's face. Where, moments before, there had been warmth and desire, now there was cool reserve.

So, he had never forgiven her. Did that mean he still felt something? Or was it just that he couldn't be content to see her again without raking her over the coals about her desertion?

Long lashes shadowed her eyes as she dropped her gaze and studied her tea. Her marriage had been a terrible mistake. It had hurt her. It had hurt Garreth. But, most of all, it had hurt Quint. She had tried to love him, but it just hadn't happened. He had become nearly obsessive with jealousy, even after the divorce.

Garreth watched Leara intently. Emotions chased one another over her face too quickly for him to decipher. Two small lines appeared between her brows and her soft lips looked pinched. Her free hand clenched and unclenched nervously. He suddenly realized that she was holding back tears behind those sheltering lashes.

Why was she suddenly so distant, trying not to cry?

He could have sworn that she was feeling the same desire he was. Was she feeling guilty because he'd reminded her about her husband?

Leara placed her glass on the end table and started to get up.

"You said you work at a day care center?" he asked, quickly changing the subject.

Leara turned overbright eyes on him and settled back into her chair. "Yes, for the last couple of years." Was he really interested in what she did for a living? Being in business hadn't been her intention when she'd gotten the job with Becky. That it had turned into a partnership in three child care centers after only two years still amazed her.

"Do you like the work?"

"Yes. I didn't realize until recently that it means the world to me. The kids are what make it so wonderful for me. They have such great imaginations. They can make the world into anything they want. Being around them, sometimes even I believe that anything is possible. And I've made some very good friends, too."

One of those friends was Theo, a child development specialist she often consulted before introducing new games and activities in the day cares. She'd been dating Theo. They had fun together and they shared a love of children, but there were no sparks between them. Maybe that was why their relationship had never gone beyond good-night kisses. She realized that this was the first time she'd thought of Theo since arriving in Columbus.

Leara rose from her chair just as Garreth reached for her hand. Avoiding his hand, she grabbed the empty glasses and headed for the kitchen. She was acutely aware that Garreth followed.

She set the glasses on the table, her back still to him. She asked the question she couldn't postpone any longer. "Why are you here, Garreth?"

He avoided it. "Do you and Quint have any children?" he asked. If they didn't, it might be easier . . .

Her back was to him as she poured more iced tea, and Leara shook her head. She had wanted a child. Quint had been adamant in his refusal. To his way of thinking, a child would have tied them down; upset the carefree life-style he preferred. They had argued about children often during their first year together. Later, when she'd realized Quint would never grow up himself, she'd stopped talking to him about it. She knew what it was like to have a father who didn't care about her. She wanted any child of hers to have two loving parents. When their relationship had gotten really rocky, she'd been glad that no children were involved.

"Garreth, why are you here?" she asked again. When he didn't answer, Leara turned.

He'd moved closer, and now he grasped her shoulders as he searched her eyes. He folded her to his chest and stroked her coppery curls, her slender back.

"I can't believe it—I feel as if we've never been apart. When I touch you, it's all there again. Can what I feel be so wrong?" he asked.

Leara wasn't certain if he was asking her, or himself.

"Ever since I found you this afternoon, I . . ." He stopped himself before he said too much. Where had his good intentions gone—the dinner invitation meant to bury old differences? Now, he recognized that he had been hoping all along Quint wasn't with Leara.

And Quint wasn't here.

A tremor of arousal shook Garreth. The warm allure of Leara's embrace created a feeling of timelessness, that the past and present were caught up together. The vortex of his desire for her drew him down into that past, this present.

Leara saw the hunger that burned golden in his eyes. Her next awareness was of his mouth, warm and firm, moving insistently over hers; the questing fire of Garreth's tongue; the rushing passion in her body. His hands left trails of flame as he stroked her shoulders, her back, the roundness of her hips.

Garreth reacquainted himself with her contours, with her fire. His panting breaths ruffled her reddish curls where his lips brushed against them. Open handed, he combed through her hair, felt the soft strands curve around his fingers as her head moved back against his palms. A wave of tenderness flowed through him as she opened her eyes and he saw the yearning shining in them.

Leara gasped as Garreth slid his hands under her T-shirt, slowly stroking her bare skin. She tossed her head back, trying to cool her flushed face. Her body burned, throbbed with a need that had consumed her so quickly she was powerless to control it.

He reveled in the sight of her. She was magnificent. Her skin was heated silk under his seeking fingers. His searching hands found her breasts, their tiny hard peaks so sensitive that she moaned when he touched her. He answered her, a growl vibrating from him as he buried his face against her neck, searing her skin with hot kisses.

"Leara!"

The single word rasped from deep within him, as though he'd struggled to suppress it. It reverberated through her where her breasts were again pressed to his chest. She quivered with the heat that penetrated where their thighs and hips were pressed together.

Leara remembered Garreth's lovemaking, their joyful explorations of each other, learning to please, to stimulate. It was something they had learned together.

But the boy Garreth was gone. The man whose passionate kisses and caresses were turning her blood to flame was more bold, more masterful than that earnest young man had been.

Garreth cupped Leara's face with trembling hands and looked into her desire-clouded eyes. He wanted her too much. He was stunned by the force of it—the need to love her, possess her. No other woman had ever made him feel like this.

He closed his eyes to block out the ardor in hers, because that ardor pressed his control to the limit. Her look incited him to give in to the emotions that swamped them both.

And he wanted to. Every nerve blazed with his need. He ached to carry her to the nearest bed, to strip them both of the frustrating clothes, to press himself against her, into her. And if he went one inch further, if she moved against him again, there'd be no holding back.

"Damn, this feels so right!" He wasn't even aware that he had spoken his thoughts aloud.

"Oh, yes." Her reply slipped from her like a sigh. All she wanted in that moment was to be joined to him, to be consumed by this fire.

Garreth caught her earlobe between his lips, nipping it lightly at the same time his callused fingertips moved across the sensitized skin of her stomach to the slight depression of her belly button. The combination shot a bolt of desire through her, robbing her of her breath, tingling her breasts and the center of her womanhood.

Experienced!

The word leapt into her brain. This wasn't her Garreth at all. This wasn't the young man with whom she had discovered love. This Garreth was arousing her skillfully, totally—soon she would have been panting for him to take her to the bedroom—and he was doing things to her that he must have learned with other women.

Like his wife.

Illogically, she felt that he had been unfaithful—as though his wife had come between them. Then, just as suddenly, she felt guilty.

Garreth felt Leara stiffen in his arms.

"No, don't pull away from me, Leara. Not now. Not after so long . . ." He captured her mouth again, kissing her fervently, desperately trying to pull them back into the past, the memories. But the magic had gone.

Reluctantly, he raised his head and loosened his hold.

"Garreth, this isn't right. We're different people than we were ten years ago, aren't we? There are other commitments to consider now, aren't there?" Her tone was bitter.

"No. It isn't right." Anger boiled up in him, giving him the strength to release her completely. "This never should have happened," he said, the words grating in his throat as he fought to control his voice. "You made your choice ten years ago."

At his accusing tone, an answering anger blazed in Leara. "We both did, didn't we?" she snapped.

Instead of getting the furious comeback she'd expected, Leara was thrown off balance when Garreth reached out and touched her cheek, stroking it gently. He looked so sad, so filled with regret.

"I guess we did," he murmured. "Even if those choices were wrong."

She stared at the old screen door long after he'd gone.

THREE

Leara cast a satisfied look at the clean living room before she closed and locked the front door. It had taken a lot of work, but the place was clean at last and ready to show to prospective buyers. She'd made an appointment with her friend Marijo, who owned a flourishing real estate agency, and was on her way now to the office to sign a sale agreement with her. Then she could leave Columbus, and all its memories, and get on with her life.

For the last two days, she'd been very busy, but Garreth had been on her mind at every turn. He hadn't been back to see her. She told herself that she was glad, but whenever she'd heard an engine stop on the street outside the house or the slam of a car door, she'd gone to the window, hoping to see Garreth striding up the walk.

I don't have the right, she reasoned. *He's married. He has other commitments.* Soon, she'd be in Gary, and Garreth would again be a part of her past.

As Leara started down the steps, the full heat of the day struck her. Though it was only June, the temperature was in the nineties. The car would be scorching. The tree-shaded park across the street almost called to Leara as she walked down the short driveway.

"What the heck, it's only three blocks," Leara muttered as she stepped into the street and started across.

Suddenly, a voice shouted her name, and the sound of squealing brakes ripped through her. Frozen by fear, she looked up in terror as a green sedan screeched to a halt, its bumper almost touching her knees. Trembling, Leara sank to the ground.

"Leara! Oh, come on! You're not hurt—I wasn't going to hit you! It was just a joke. . . ."

The voice was familiar, but Leara was still too stunned to focus on it. She was busy trying to get her heart back in her chest and her breathing back to normal. She felt someone lift her. She tried to clear her vision enough to make out who carried her to the curb. Then he set her on her feet. For a few seconds the face didn't register. She still gripped the man's arms, her knees shaky.

Leara snatched her hands away as she realized who held her. "Quint." The word expressed all the disapproval and irritation that the sight of her ex-husband evoked in her. "What the hell are you doing here?"

"Ah, c'mon, Leara. I wasn't trying to scare you. I just—uh—happened to be passing and saw you crossing the street. It was just a prank. Really."

Leara shook his hand off and leaned over to brush the road grit from her bare legs, checking for damage to her dress and sandals. She straightened, hands on her hips, and surveyed her ex-husband.

He hadn't changed much. His clothes looked more expensive. His blond hair was just a little too long, his smile just a little too bright. And that stance—well, he'd always been arrogant. She couldn't understand, now, what it was about him that had attracted her.

But he had been attractive, perhaps because he'd been reckless.

"You didn't answer my question," she reminded him.

"I told you, I was just passing by. I pass here every day on my way to the dealership. I saw you crossing the street. It was an impulse. Just a crazy joke."

"It was stupid and dangerous. Your brakes could have failed!" This didn't seem to affect him. "Why aren't you in Gary? You aren't—"

She'd been about to accuse him of following her, as he had when they'd first separated. But she bit back the accusation.

"I had a better offer, so I'm back in the old hometown. I'm half owner of a new dealership over on Preston Street." His careless grin oozed charm, but Leara wasn't buying it. He might have injured her severely with his stupid stunt.

What is this, anyway—old home week? Leara thought in dismay. First she'd run into Garreth, and now Quint had almost literally run into her.

She had to wonder, though, if Quint's appearance was more than coincidence. Just last month, he'd sent her a birthday card and flowers. And it wouldn't be the first time that he'd followed her. When they'd first separated, he'd popped up every time she turned around.

"Look," he told her, "I'm sorry I frightened you. I admit, it was stupid. But, I really didn't mean anything by it. Forgive me?"

"Okay, Quint. I have to go." Smoothing her hair with her hands, Leara turned toward the park.

"Where are you going?" Quint asked, grabbing her hand and pulling her around to face him again. "I'd be glad to give you a ride."

"No thanks. I'm going to Marijo's office. It's just down the street."

Leara smiled as Quint frowned. Marijo Gordon had been her best friend in high school, but Quint and Marijo had always had an active dislike for one another—a dislike that turned loud and vocal whenever the two happened to meet. After Leara and Quint had married, it had been impossible for her to maintain her close friendship with Marijo. Quint's jealousy had interfered.

Her relationship with Marijo had dwindled to Christmas cards crammed with pictures and long letters about the year's happenings. But since the divorce, Marijo was her best friend again.

"You're going to M.J.'s? Just a visit, or are you buying? You coming back to Columbus for good, Lea? I thought you were happy in Gary, what with your day care business raking it in."

Leara pushed down her irritation. Quint made it sound as if she was only interested in the money the centers brought in.

"I am happy there. But, then, you know that. No, I'm going to put Gram's house up for sale. Dad left it to me."

"Yeah? I heard he died. Sorry." He looked back at the white wood-frame house. "So, he didn't disown you completely. How much does M.J. think it will bring?"

"Thanks for your condolences." Her tone was bitter.

"C'mon Leara. Don't tell me you're all broke up about it. It's not like the major ever gave a damn about you."

Leara flinched at the remark.

She'd been hurt—terribly hurt—when her father had disowned her, never answering her letters, hanging up whenever she'd tried to call. Quint hadn't shown much sympathy then. Looking back on their life together, she suspected that Quint had never wanted to share her attention with anyone. He'd always needed an adoring follower to boost his ego. Someone to impress. The strange thing was, she had never been able to admire him the way he seemed to need her to. And the more he tried to impress her with his grand schemes and risky deals, which invariably fell through, the less she was impressed.

And her memories of Garreth had stood between them.

She supposed she must have been a disappointment to Quint, too. Maybe that was why, in the end, he had turned to other women.

Leara tried to ease her fingers from Quint's grip, but he held on tighter. Long, almost girlish lashes lowered over his blue eyes as he looked at her. *Why, he's flirting with me!* she thought in surprise.

"Come on, Lea, let me drive you to M.J.'s," he pleaded. "I just want to talk to you for a minute."

"You know we have nothing to talk about."

"Not even old times?" Quint asked, flashing his most engaging grin.

"Old times? Old times like Rosemary? Or Sheila—?"

"Okay, Lea. I know you don't trust me, Lea. But, I've changed. Really I have."

He sounded as though he meant it, as though he might have grown up at last. Well, she hoped so for his sake. She was familiar with Quint's talent for false sincerity, which was what made him such a good car salesman. It put a question mark on everything he said.

Quint squeezed her hand. "Can't we at least be friends?"

"I'll think about it," she said. She pulled her hand free from his. "Thanks for the offer of a ride, but I'm going to walk to Marijo's."

"Okay, Lea. Look me up. I'm in the book." He

gave her a swift kiss on the cheek and headed for his car.

Leara walked slowly through the park, thinking about the encounter and wondering what Quint was up to. She felt a familiar pang of guilt. She had always known it wasn't really Quint's fault that their marriage hadn't worked. Quint had known it, too—known that in Leara's heart she'd never loved him, or accepted him for what he was. Though she'd tried to banish thoughts of Garreth, he'd always been there, like a shadow between them.

Mr. Perfect, Quint had called him scathingly. Whenever one of Quint's schemes fell through, he would say bitterly, "I suppose Mr. Perfect would have done better?"

She had tried to be the attentive, dutiful wife that Quint seemed to want. Her memories of Garreth had gradually faded, but her marriage had failed anyway. Leara knew now that it had been doomed from the start—probably would have been even if she had never met Garreth Conroe.

Leara pushed thoughts of the past away and turned her attention to the sounds of laughter coming from the playground near the opposite corner of the park. The sun, as it flickered through the gaps in the tree branches, lighted the little heads as the children ran. The music of their voices soothed her, reminding her that she had a satisfying life elsewhere: in Gary, at the day care centers, working with her kids. She no longer needed to be an extension of someone else—someone's girlfriend, someone's wife. She had her own identity and she liked who she was. If her life wasn't perfect, well, nobody's life was perfect. And there was still the future. Time for marriage and her own children.

Her past with Garreth, her marriage to Quint were

history. Maybe Garreth realized that now. Maybe that was why he hadn't been back.

"Leara! *Niña!*" Marijo Gordon rushed across the outer office of MJ Realty and hugged Leara enthusiastically.

Maria Josephina Chavez had been the first friend Leara had made when she'd come to Columbus. Marijo had been a newcomer, too. Her father, who worked for Cummins Engines, had been transferred from Cummins' New Mexico plant. They had seemed to naturally gravitate toward one another.

"It's so good to see you again!" Holding Leara at arm's length, Marijo looked her up and down.

"You look terrific, M.J. Success obviously agrees with you." Leara indicated the half-dozen agents—working at desks, talking to clients, or speaking on the phones—all of whom worked for her friend.

"How long has it been since we last got together, anyway?"

"Almost two years—since I came down for Kimmi's eighth birthday."

"C'mon in my office. I'm dying to catch up," Marijo said. She led Leara into a large, less formally decorated inner office. Rose pink accordion-pleated shades muted the strong light from the windows into a rosy glow. Lush potted palms and ferns filled the corners. Graceful angelfish swam in slow circles in a large aquarium against the wall.

Once Leara was seated on a comfortable loose-cushioned sofa, sipping a cup of coffee, Marijo searched her face, "Why is there dirt on your knees?"

Leara smiled ruefully. "I just ran into Quint. Or, I should say, he nearly ran into me!" She told Marijo about the meeting.

"That sounds like something Quint would do," Marijo snorted. "I'd heard he was back in town. What you ever saw in him! Sure, he's a hunk, and I know you dated him for a while before Garreth came along, but then to throw over Garreth for that irresponsible—"

"M.J., my problems with Quint weren't all his fault," Leara cut in. "Sometimes I think, well, I think that if I could have just believed in him—"

"Oh, come on, Leara! I know you always want to see the best in people, but let's be realistic. Quint is one leopard who'll never change his spots."

"I suppose you're right. But let's talk about something else—like your business. This new office is impressive!"

"Oh, business is fair, considering how soft the market is right now," Marijo said. "It may take some time to sell your grandmother's house."

"Fair? I've heard yours is the busiest real estate office in this part of Indiana. Really, M.J., are you sure you want to handle a small property like Gram's house? It looks like you have bigger projects to deal with." Leara indicated an architect's model of a large complex. "What's this?"

"Like it?" Marijo asked. "It's the new mall that's going up out on Trenton Road. Garreth Conroe designed it." There was a curious gleam in her eye as she studied Leara. "He's back in Columbus, you know."

"Yes, I know. I ran into him at Ferguson's Market." She tried to make her voice sound calm, uninterested. "He . . . hasn't changed much."

He hadn't changed at all—he'd only gotten to me more: more handsome, more successful, more . . . married.

"Oh, really?" Marijo's tone was plainly speculative. "You spoke to him? Was he glad to see you?"

"Yes, M.J., we talked. After all, we are old friends."

"Oh, come on, Lea! You and Garreth were never just friends."

"That was ten years ago, Marijo. We have some good memories—and some bad ones. That's all. Besides, it's a moot point. He's married. He has a child."

"Poor Garreth was never really married. He didn't tell you about his wife? C'mon, Leara. You don't have the whole story. You know, Garreth was—"

"M.J.! I don't want to discuss him."

"But, Lea—"

"No!"

"Lea—"

"Enough!"

"Okay! Okay! I surrender!" Marijo's black eyes flashed with exasperation. "You know, Leara, you're just as stubborn as always! All right. Garreth's name will not pass my lips again unless you bring up the subject. Okay?"

"Okay."

"Now, let's get this paperwork out of the way. I already have a couple of prospects looking for a place like your grandmother's. Tell you what, why don't you come over to my place for supper tonight? I'm making Chimichanga casserole. It used to be your favorite of my mom's dishes when you'd sleep over. I can pick you up when I come by to see the house at four thirty. You can see Kimmi and Bill, and we can talk some more."

"A real meal sounds great. I brought my little microwave to Gram's. I've been existing mainly on TV dinners. Even when I'm at home, I don't have much interest in cooking. Seems kind of pointless when it's just for one."

"Well, we'll just have to see about fixing that. It's time you got involved again." Marijo pointed to a line on the sales agreement.

Leara shook her head and signed the papers. "No thank you."

"That smells delicious!" Leara said as she gathered the salad vegetables she'd just washed into a large pottery bowl and carried them to the island workstation in the center of M.J.'s kitchen. It was a warm room. Loads of sunlight streamed in through the wide windows framed by cheerful red and white gingham curtains. Pots of bright red geraniums and white begonias were displayed on the windowsill and on a wrought-iron baker's rack. The white plaster walls, exposed beams, and terra cotta tile reflected M.J.'s Mexican American heritage, but the brightly polished cookware, ropes of garlic, strings of bright red chili peppers, and bunches of dried herbs hanging from racks overhead were functional as well as decorative. Leara grabbed a knife from the slotted rack built into the corner of the butcher block top and began cutting tomatoes into wedges. "What do you call that, anyway?"

"Try sautéed onions," Marijo laughed, giving the pan a final stir with a wooden spoon before taking it off the heat. "Why haven't you answered your invitation for the class reunion? Terri told me she hasn't heard from you. You didn't come to the five-year reunion. You really should make the ten-year."

"I don't know. Why do people go to those things anyway? Just to see if they're more successful than everyone else, or to see if that miserable Laurie Ashworth, who edged me out of homecoming queen, has gotten fat as a cow and that dark fuzz on her upper lip has developed into a full-grown mustache?"

"You've got it! So are you going?"

Leara hadn't really considered it. If she were honest with herself, she admitted, the thought of rehashing old times just didn't appeal to her. Her old times had centered on Garreth.

"Quint didn't want to go to the five-year reunion."

As she folded a layer of flour tortillas into the casserole dish, Marijo said, "You avoided my question, Lea. What's so traumatic about a picnic with a few old friends? You wouldn't have to go to the dance that night—unless you wanted to. You'll get to see who's divorced and who's remarried—and who's divorced and remarried again. Like Fred Luntz. He's going on his fourth."

Leara sensed that tidbit was designed to put her at ease, if her reason for wanting to avoid the reunion was that she felt that everyone would be speculating about her divorce.

"C'mon, Leara. What's the real reason? And don't tell me it's because Quint's going to be there. I know better."

Leara grimaced. "There are only a few people from our class that I'd like to see. I can do that without going to some stupid picnic and watching everyone pretend they're still eighteen." Leara wiped her hands on a towel and smoothed the apron over her white eyelet sundress. After days in grubby jeans and shorts, wearing a dress and makeup made her feel feminine again.

"Salad's done. What's next?"

Marijo's answer was forestalled as a bundle of energy topped by bouncing black curls and a baseball cap blew in through the dining room door.

"Hey, Mom! Coach is coming to dinner. We're late 'cause I had to stop by the library after practice, so I could finish that report. Imagine a summer school teacher assigning— *Aunt Leara!*"

Kimmi launched herself at Leara, who caught her in a hug.

"My, you've grown!" Leara laughed as she was almost bowled over.

"Aunt Leara, it's been ages and ages since you came to see us!"

"I've been working a lot. I see you like the present I sent for your birthday."

"You know it!" Kimmi snatched off her Chicago Cubs cap, which had been autographed by her favorite player. "I can't believe you actually talked to Luis Salazar!"

"He said that he was glad to autograph a cap for a fellow third baseman."

"Did you tell him I'm his biggest fan ever?"

"Sure did."

"I think he's kind of cute, too, for an old guy. Did he ask you for a date?" Kimmi's impish grin disappeared as she ducked Leara's swat.

"*Niña,* go upstairs and get a shower before supper." Marijo wrinkled her nose expressively as her daughter passed by. "Hurry now. You can talk to Leara after you clean up and change."

"Okay, Mom. But first I want to know if Aunt Leara can come to my game tomorrow." She turned to Leara. "Please, will you? If I get two more hits, I'll take the lead in hitting in my league for all of Columbus!" Kimmi said excitedly.

"Sure. I'd love to come watch."

"Great!"

"Like mother, like daughter," Leara commented as Kimmi bounced out. Marijo just smirked.

Leara placed the salad in the refrigerator. "I'm going to set the table," she said as she shut the refrigerator door. "Did you want to serve wine? Or iced tea?"

"Why not have wine? The glasses are on the sideboard in the dining room," Marijo said, then smiled and winked at someone behind Leara. "Hello, Coach. Glad you could have dinner with us."

Leara had a funny sinking feeling. She turned and found Garreth's tall frame in the doorway. His dark blue blazer emphasized his wide shoulders. His baby blue shirt, open at the collar, showed the strong column of his throat. His dark hair curled boyishly across his forehead, but his brown eyes were shadowed, reserved. His expression was unreadable.

"Hello," he told Leara softly.

"Garreth, when you ran into Leara the other day, why didn't you tell her that you've been divorced for nearly as long as she has?" Marijo asked as she shoved the casserole into the oven.

Garreth straightened suddenly, his expression intense. His eyes were only for Leara as he unconsciously took a step toward her. "Why didn't you tell me? If I had known . . ."

Leara felt as if she'd been turned to stone. Garreth wasn't married? He was free? That should have made her ecstatic. Why did it scare the hell out of her instead?

" 'Garreth, why don't you drive Leara back to her grandmother's house? She came with me, so she doesn't have her car,' " Leara mimicked Marijo as Garreth's car sped through the dark Midwest night. "I've seen subtler freight trains," she added, looking out the window at the lights of houses they passed. "I wondered at the time why Marijo insisted that I leave my car at Gram's house when her house is so far out of town and it would have been really inconvenient for her to drive me back."

"Don't worry about it," Garreth murmured. Marijo and Bill had carried most of the table conversation during dinner. Leara had talked more with Kimmi than with the adults, avoiding Garreth's eyes. Now, he glanced at the woman beside him, noting the tenseness in the set of her shoulders, the way her fingers clasped and unclasped in her lap. He sighed. "I saw that killer look you sent M.J. and I realized you weren't too happy about me driving you home."

"Oh, I'm sorry! I don't mean to be ungrateful. It's just . . ." The irritation she'd felt building all evening suddenly boiled out in a rush of words. "I *don't* like to be manipulated!"

A few moments of silence followed, broken only by the hum of the engine and the radio playing softly. Then Garreth said quietly, "I'm a little slow, Leara. I was so happy to learn that you're not with Quint, it took me until M.J.'s chocolate pound cake to realize that you weren't thrilled that I'm free, too. Is . . . there someone else? Is that why you've been so reserved? Or, . . . or, dammit! Are you still in love with Quint?"

His profile, etched in the half light from the dash, was all harsh angles. Leara's anger at M.J.'s machinations drained away.

"There's no one. I . . ." She'd been about to tell him that she'd never loved Quint, but the words stuck in her throat. Because she'd never loved Quint as he'd wanted her to, her actions that long ago June night, a night so much like this one, seemed all the more unforgivable. She'd used one man's love selfishly and broken another's heart. Now, she was amazed that Garreth didn't hate her for it.

Leara started to touch his cheek, to smooth the wrinkles from his forehead, to tell him "I'm sorry!" as she'd wanted to tell him so many times through the years. The hand she'd lifted dropped to her lap and she turned back to the window and the Midwest summer night.

"I just seem to have lost the ability to make normal conversation this evening," she said.

Garreth drew in a deep breath and realized in surprise that he was gripping the steering wheel so tightly his fingers were starting to cramp. Smiling ruefully, he flexed them. "We used to talk for hours," he mused. He lifted her hand from her lap and wrapped it in his large one, surprised to find it cold. "And . . . other things, Cinderella."

He was so familiar—the way his smile lifted more at one corner of his mouth than the other, the warm timbre of his voice. He was the same man she hadn't been able to forget, even in those early years when she'd tried desperately to put what they'd shared behind her and make her marriage to Quint Lockwood work.

But this Garreth was different, too. In so many ways a stranger. Darkly handsome. Poised. At ease and un-impressed with himself as he guided his sleek Mercedes through the night. He was no longer the college student who'd planned his future so carefully. Those plans had obviously come to fruition; even so, the look deep in his warm brown eyes was faintly self-mocking. The dinner table conversation—as M.J. had no doubt made certain—revealed that Garreth was now a full partner in a successful architectural firm. He'd been married, too. And he had a daughter.

As the car approached the intersection, which would take them back to Columbus, Garreth made a decision and turned onto a road he hadn't taken for ten years.

Suddenly, Leara realized that they were going the wrong way. "Garreth, what are you doing? This isn't the way home." As he made a left turn onto a narrow gravel track, she caught her breath. "This is the way to Tarzan's Lake!"

"We have to talk. What is it? I've felt you pulling away all evening. If there's no one else, then what's wrong, Cinderella?'' Garreth demanded as he stopped the car and cut the engine. The quiet was sudden. Enveloping.

"I'm not your 'Cinderella' anymore. Just because there's no one else in my life at the moment doesn't mean that there aren't problems. We've made different lives. We don't have the same dreams anymore.''

"We had the same dream once. We can find it again.''

"I gave up that dream, Garreth. And I grew up. Life isn't 'happily ever after' with Prince Charming on a white charger. Anyway, white chargers can make for a damned bumpy ride.''

"I know life isn't a fairy tale. But, what we had is as close as anyone gets. We were happy—''

"Happiness is relative,'' Leara cut in. "In my life now, I may not have the terrific highs, but I don't have the devastating lows, either. I have peace, and a feeling of accomplishment.''

He was silent for a moment, looking out at the darkness. "I never thought you would be the one to compromise. That was more my speed.''

"Garreth, I—'' she began, about to tell him that she had always compromised, had always let what someone else wanted shape her dreams. Her father, Garreth, Quint—they had all come first, until a couple of years ago when she'd finally taken responsibility for her own life. But as she turned to him, Garreth's strong fingers touched her cheek. His touch stunned her, taking away her ability to speak, to think. As he cupped her cheek lightly and gently stroked her bottom lip with his thumb, she was held immobile.

"Are you happy, Leara? Can you tell me you're happy, like we were back then?'' His dark eyes searched hers. "We were just kids; we didn't even know what we had! Did you ever find anything that even came close? I didn't. I didn't, and God knows, I looked hard enough.

"If someone had asked me if I was happy before I walked into Ferguson's Market a couple of days ago, I might have rationalized about highs and lows and feelings of accomplishment, but the truth is there's been a hole in my life since the day you left. I'd just learned to ignore it. Filled it with work, with other women, with marriage to someone else. Out of all of it, being a parent has been the most rewarding—but the hole is still there. If I'd never seen you again, I might even have gone on believing that I was happy. But after holding you in my arms again, I stood on the edge of that very big, deep hole and wondered how I had ever ignored it."

His deep voice caressed her. His intensity as he spoke was mesmerizing. Leara felt herself being drawn toward him, as much by the compelling words and look in his eyes as the gentle pressure of his fingers. In another instant, she'd be in his arms.

"I can't think straight when you're this close!" Leara gasped, pulling away before he could kiss her. She shoved the car door open and escaped into the warm June night.

Thousands of crickets played their shrill songs, vying with the cicadas up in the trees. The thick blanket of leaves under the trees permeated the air with a sweet earthy smell. The half-moon offered little light as Leara, ignoring Garreth's calls for her to wait, crossed the railroad tracks that ran parallel to the highway. She disappeared on the other side between the two oaks that marked the path to the small lake she remembered all too well.

It only took seconds to break out of the trees onto the sandy bank. Startled at the human intrusion, dozens of frogs sitting in the shadows stopped their love choruses and dove for safety, punctuating the night with a series of watery plops.

"Leara!" Garreth caught her shoulders and turned her around. Beneath his straight brows, his eyes shone in the near darkness. His voice seemed to come from far away. "I brought you here because this was where we always came to talk. Here, the rest of the world faded into the background and we could work out our problems."

Yes, she remembered. Together, they had discovered this hidden pond, within its sheltering woods. It had been a secret refuge for her and her teenaged friends; a place where they could be free of responsibilities. She remembered the beauty, the peace, the solitude. She had come here to unravel the tangles in her life. And to experience love.

This was the place of her awakening, where they had made love that first time. This sand had cradled them, these trees had witnessed their promises of devotion. This moon had bathed them in a glow that had never faded from memory.

Now, it was suddenly all there again. Garreth's face was as stark with hunger as it had been that warm June night long ago. Leara wanted to look away, to break the strange spell the moonlight was casting, but she felt herself moving toward him instead. A whirlpool of wanting flooded her.

"Leara," he said huskily. "You're still so beautiful—I was such a fool!" Her face was in shadow, but her eyes glowed softly in the faint light from the stars and the pale half-moon. They cast a silvery sheen on her hair and reflected in ripples on the lake. Her white dress stood out stark against the dark background of the water. She looked ethereal in the darkness, like an illusion he was trying to grasp.

Cradling her face in his hands, Garreth kissed her

gently, almost reverently. Leara shivered and tilted her head back, opening her mouth to him. Groaning, Garreth deepened the kiss, molding her warmth against his long frame. His tongue thrust into her mouth in a primitive supplication. In answer, she pressed herself even closer to his hardness, her hands exploring the muscles of his back beneath his blazer. In response, Garreth growled against her neck and caught her bottom, pressing her more firmly against his arousal.

Leara moaned, her heart pounding as if trying to free itself from her body. Then Garreth cupped her breast through the cotton eyelet of her sundress, and her heart broke free and took flight.

Garreth pulled away, and taking off his blazer, he spread it on the sand. Then he was kissing her again and lowering her to the ground. The touch of Garreth's fingers was gentle as he slid the strap of her dress from her shoulders. He kissed a path down her neck and lower, his lips blessing each new inch of skin exposed on the mounds of her breasts as his hands tugged her dress lower.

The moonlight, the sand beneath her outstretched hand, Garreth's shadowed face tight with passion—she had lived it all before. The sameness startled her, clearing her passion-drugged mind. She caught his hands. "What's happening, Garreth? Are we both trying to recapture what we once shared? Is that it?"

Garreth lifted himself on his elbows. "Is that so wrong?"

"This isn't real. It's just old memories."

"What I feel *is* real, Leara. It hasn't changed. Now that I've found you again, there has to be a chance for us to make it work."

"I have my life in Gary, you have your life here. You have a child—how can it be the same?"

"Are you telling me that you don't feel anything anymore?" he asked quietly.

Leara looked up into his eyes, burning in the darkness, and shook her head. "I feel too much! That's what frightens me; that's what makes me think it can't be real. It's too much, too fast—we really don't know each other anymore! It can't be the same!"

"Then give it time. Trust me. Give me time. I know that's all we need to find it again."

"I'll try," she whispered, half frightened at what she was promising. Suddenly, Leara realized the problem was that she wasn't at all sure she wanted to recapture the past.

Garreth helped her up and retrieved his blazer. He turned toward her, his smile tentative. "I want to be with you tomorrow, but my Little League team has a game. Come with me?"

"Okay." She'd told Kimmi she'd go, anyway. Maybe he was right, Leara thought as Garreth placed his arm around her shoulders and they started back to the car.

FOUR

"Headache!"

The cry startled Leara. It was the top of the third inning, with one man on base, one out. The game was all tied up at one run each. Leara sat in the bleachers behind the batter's box. She'd been half turned around, listening to Marijo chatter about the strengths and weaknesses of the Red Sox, the team opposing Garreth's Athletics. Now, as Leara looked at the people around her clasping their arms protectively over their heads, she couldn't imagine what was going on.

A baseball, fouled back over the protective wire netting behind the batter's box, bounced in the dust in front of the bleachers. Leara suddenly remembered the meaning of "Headache!" when yelled during a baseball game. She caught the ball reflexively as it headed straight for her nose.

"Nice catch, Aunt Leara!" Kimmi, who'd run up from her position on third base to try to make the play, grinned approvingly.

"Uh, thanks," Leara muttered, thinking no one could have been more surprised than she at the feat.

As she tossed the ball back over the wire screen to Kimmi, she saw Garreth smiling at her. She smiled back, thinking how different he looked—younger, more relaxed—in his baseball cap, A's T-shirt, and jeans. He was more like the younger Garreth she had known. She warmed at the look he gave her.

"Looks like Coach has his eye on you," commented Sandra, a petite brunette who'd introduced herself earlier as the mother of the A's catcher.

"They came together," supplied a blonde on the top row. "Hello," she said to Leara, leaning forward and extending her hand. "I'm Carol Flanders. The left fielder's mine."

"Leara Lockwood." She stretched and shook Carol's hand as the pitcher wound up and delivered. The umpire called "Ball!"

"So, have you known Garreth long?" asked Carol in the relative silence following the call.

"Girl, you're about as subtle as a train wreck," laughed a slender black woman seated on the tier below Leara. She extended her hand. "Amy Whitman," she said, her liquid black eyes dancing with merriment. "Amy Lowell Whitman. The second baseman is my nephew."

"Hello. I'm— Amy Lowell? Is that you? Why didn't you say something? You've changed so much! I'd never have recognized you!" Leara clasped her hand warmly. In high school they'd been in the same home economics class.

"About forty pounds worth of change. I made Marijo promise not to give me away, to see if you'd recognize me. You look the same, girl. When I saw you walking with Garreth earlier, I thought I'd taken a step ten years straight back in time to high school."

"Not quite the same. I do have one or two gray hairs," Leara smiled ruefully.

"That's my husband, George, over by the concession stand. I'll introduce you later." Amy continued in the nonstop fashion that Leara remembered well, "So, are you back in Columbus permanently? Marijo told me that you and Quint were divorced." Amy looked pointedly from Leara to where Garreth stood in the A's dugout. "I always thought you two would end up together. Well?"

"I . . . I . . . ," Leara didn't know what to say. She'd spent an almost sleepless night, thinking, wondering if they really could pick up where they'd left off, as if ten years hadn't passed. She'd come to the very sensible conclusion that they were in danger of mistaking nostalgia for love and being swept away by passion left over from ten years ago. She'd decided that, no matter how strong the chemistry between them, she wouldn't rush into anything. She had decided to insist that they take it slowly and carefully.

Then, when Garreth had come to pick her up that morning, he'd wrapped her in his arms, and his kiss had been deep and devastating, shattering into a million fragments all the sensible resolutions that she'd made in the small hours before dawn. In his arms, it was easy to believe that they could just pick up where they'd left off and live happily ever after.

"I'm not here permanently," Leara began. "I have a day care business in Gary, and—"

"You're coming back for the class reunion, though, aren't you?" Amy asked.

"Yes, she'll be here for the class reunion," Marijo inserted, her face the picture of innocence—just as if Leara hadn't offered a dozen excuses the night before.

"That's great, Leara," said Amy. "I love the idea of an afternoon picnic, so the children won't be left out. I'm looking forward to that more than the dance that evening. Seeing everyone again will be fun."

Seeing everyone else's family wouldn't be. That was the main reason Leara found the thought of a class reunion unappealing. She knew people would ask about her family, and she'd have to smile and explain. Twenty-eight and single. In high school she'd imagined something very different for herself ten years down the road. When she'd dreamed of her future, it had always been as Garreth's wife.

And now, incredibly, Garreth said he wanted to be in her life again. So, what was wrong? Why did this little warning bell keep going off in her head?

Leara sighed and searched her mind for a plausible excuse for missing the reunion. She couldn't think of any.

The umpire called another ball and gave the sign for a full count. Everyone around her, including Amy, was suddenly focused on the game, shouting advice and encouragement to the team.

The pitcher wound up and delivered again. Another ball, and the batter walked. The Athletics' fans groaned as the Sox's fans cheered.

Marijo jumped to her feet. "Who wants to contribute to the fund for blind umpires?" she yelled out. "I'm taking up a collection to get Bob the new pair of glasses he needs so much!"

Several people in the bleachers waved dollar bills and laughed. Bill patiently ignored his wife's outburst.

As Garreth went out to the mound to steady his pitcher, Leara admired his relaxed attitude, the way he seemed to impart quiet confidence to the ten-year-old on the mound, who now had to be feeling a ton of pressure.

The next batter up popped out.

"Leara, I left my three-year-old down at the other end of the bleachers playing with Robert and Chelsea's little girl—their son is right field," Amy said. "You remember them, don't you—Robert Nations and Chelsea Binton? There are one or two others here, too, from the old gang. I'd better go before Georgie starts sawing down the bleachers.''

"I'll walk with you, if you don't mind," Leara said, rising.

They found Amy's son carefully placing a paper soft drink cup upside down in the dust, a very solemn expression on his face. He then stomped it flat, clapped his hands, and laughed. A little girl of about the same age set a cup beside his flat one. He stomped her cup, too, and she gave him a shove for his trouble. Georgie ended up on his bottom beside the squashed cups.

As Amy dusted off her son, Leara found several other people she'd known in high school. Robert, who'd been the class clown, was soon regaling them with a hilarious account of some of his early med school days. He was now a first-year resident at the hospital. He was in the middle of a disappearing-cadaver story when Leara heard a high-pitched voice she recognized.

"There she is! There she is! That's daddy's friend!"

Leara turned, smiling. Her smile faltered when she saw that Jenny had in tow one of the most beautiful women Leara had ever seen. Leara's gaze went from Jenny to the woman, who looked to be in her mid-twenties. Her ash blond hair was several shades darker than the little girl's; probably the shade Jenny's would become. The woman's eyes were green, not Jenny's sparkling sherry brown, but there was a definite similarity in the bone structure of their faces and in their smiles.

Leara stuck out her hand, a little uncertain. "Hi. I'm Leara. And I'm confused. Garreth said his assistant would drop Jenny off."

"I'm Teresa, his assistant." She shook Leara's hand,

then she ruffled Jenny's curls. "I'm also this munch-kin's aunt. I know—we look alike. Marlene, her mother, is my sister."

"She could be yours," Leara said.

Teresa smiled, then looked at Leara uncertainly. "Are you sure keeping Jenny isn't a problem? Jenny and I usually watch the game together. My fiancé is waiting in the car. I guess Garreth just assumed I'd be available to take care of her, and it's her nanny's day off."

"Don't worry about anything. I'm used to taking care of children. And I'm looking forward to spending some time with Jenny." Then to Jenny, "I think you and I are going to be friends. At least, I hope so." Leara patted the space beside her on the second row.

Jenny, smiled shyly, climbed up and took a seat. "Bye, Aunt Tee Dee."

"See you later." Teresa smiled and hurried away.

A few minutes later, Leara noticed that Jenny was watching Robert's daughter and Georgie, who had re-sumed their crush-the-cup game. A rather wistful ex-pression was on her face.

"I don't think those guys would mind if you joined in," Leara said.

Jenny seemed to consider it gravely, then shook her head. "The dust comes out when you step on it, see?" she said as Georgia smashed one, "and my new socks might get dirty. See my socks?" Jenny held her feet out to show off bright purple socks trimmed with fluo-rescent pink hearts. She was dressed neatly in a crisply pressed pink shorts set and had a bright purple ribbon threaded through her hair.

"Very nice." Leara smiled at the little girl's obvious pride in her stylish appearance. "It's hot. Would you like an ice cream bar?"

Jenny considered the offer, then shook her head. "I

might get a drip. Last time I had ice cream, I got a drip, right here." She pointed beside her second button. "And Mrs. Teagle fussed at me."

"Who's Mrs. Teagle?"

"My nanny. She takes care of me while Daddy works."

"Oh." Leara noticed for the first time that Jenny wasn't just neat—the child was immaculate! No normal four-year-old should stay so neat! she thought. No, a preschooler should be running, playing, taking in the world with other children, learning to be social. Not sitting in the bleachers, staying neat.

Jenny was watching Georgie and company. Two more preschoolers had joined the original cup crushers, and there was a very serious debate going on about who should be next to stomp one of the paper cups waiting upside down in the dust. Eventually, Robert's daughter succeeded in convincing Georgie, who was much larger, that it should be her turn. The little girl took great joy in stomping it, jumping up and down on it several times after it was flat, just for good measure.

Watching the exhibition, Jenny smiled and clapped.

"That can't be much fun," Leara remarked casually.

"It looks like fun," Jenny said.

"What could be fun about it? When you step on the cup and it goes 'whoosh!' and all that dust flies up?"

Jenny nodded vigorously.

"Even if it gets on socks?"

Jenny paused, her expression thoughtful.

"You know what, Jenny? I just noticed that your socks and your clothes are all washable. You put them in the washer when they're dirty, and they come out clean."

Jenny looked up at Leara, her expression brightening.

"You could go over there and ask if you can play, too. I'd watch you to make sure you'll be okay."

The little girl thought about it, clasping her hands in her lap and swinging her feet back and forth vigorously. At length, she murmured, "They probably won't want me to play with them."

"You could go and ask."

"But what if they say no?"

"Then say, 'But I really, really want to play!' You'll never find out if they want you to play unless you go."

Leara watched as Jenny went over and talked to Robert's daughter. The pair were soon laughing together as the group began a new game: chase Georgie.

Leara saw that Garreth was welcoming his team off the field with "Good jobs" and pats on the back. She hadn't noticed when the A's had gotten the last out on the Sox. He seemed to have such a natural way with kids; she'd always thought he'd make a terrific father. Could he be missing something important with his own child?

By the time the seventh inning stretch came around, the smaller children, tired from the heat and hard play, gravitated to where Leara sat in the stands. Jenny, worn out from a vigorous game of chase, sat beside Leara, leaning against her tiredly. Smiling, Leara stroked Jenny's hair as she entertained everyone with a story.

"You do that so well," Amy commented when Leara had finished. "You even held Georgie's attention—until he nodded off." The plump preschoooler dozed contentedly on his mother's shoulder.

Leara smiled. "Remember, playing with children is what I do. Our day care centers take care of about two hundred kids, from infant to five, and there are many more in our after-school section."

"We pulled Amelia out of her day care center," Chelsea said, "because we found that there were too many kids per worker. And Amelia told us that Mrs. Brown, the woman in charge, was always fussing at everyone to get in line, sit down, take their naps, and so on. Amelia hated it there."

"I can imagine," said Leara emphatically. Too many people believed that the most important thing a preschooler could learn was discipline and that the only way to teach it to them was to crush their natural exuberance and curiosity.

"Our centers have a better ratio of workers to children than the state requires. Our workers are very carefully screened. They have to undergo a psychological screening before we even consider them for employment." She remembered the one man just this past week who'd seemed perfect for the job but who had gotten loud and threatening when he'd failed the psych tests. "But I'm afraid not everyone likes the way we operate. You see, I believe in letting kids be kids."

"What we need is for Leara to expand her business to Columbus and open a new center!" Chelsea said.

Amy nodded. "I have good day care through work—I've clawed my way up to middle management at the plant where I work. But if you'd open a good facility here, Leara, you'd make money."

"Better than that, you'd fill a real need!" Chelsea said. "Think about it?"

Leara shrugged noncommittally, not knowing what to say.

Just last week, Becky Taylor, her business partner, had mentioned that expanding their business before the end of the year would create a tax break for them.

Garreth stood in the dugout, one foot propped on the bench, his cap pulled low on his forehead as he watched the action. Her lips softened as she remembered how his mouth had felt as it moved over hers that morning. Maybe she and Becky could open a center here in Columbus, and she could move back here to run it. She could always commute back to Gary a couple of times a week to see that things were running smoothly in the centers there—much as she currently divided her time between the three right now. It would let her and Garreth have time together to rediscover each other. Maybe it would work . . .

And maybe I would move back here and things wouldn't work out with Garreth. After all, if he'd really loved me ten years ago, would he have let me go?

It was the bottom of the ninth when the A's broke loose, scoring two runs to tie the score. Leara stood Jenny on the bleachers beside her so that she could see the action as everyone cheered on the team.

"Whack it, Chase! Put it over the left field wall!" Marijo yelled. Standing on the top bleacher, she was easily heard over the rest of the crowd.

"Yeah, Chase! Hit it!" Jenny echoed, and Leara grinned as she gripped the waistband of Jenny's shorts as the girl bounced up and down on the bench.

Chase walloped the first pitch, sending a high fly deep to left field, and took off. Miraculously, the left fielder dropped the catch and the ball took a corkscrew bounce, rolling into the very corner of the playing field. Looking over his shoulder as he rounded second, Chase saw the drop and churned past third for home, the A's fans cheering wildly.

But as Chase slid for home, the catcher stepped forward, trying to catch the ball, which the fielder had thrown a little short. Dust swirled as both players ended up in a tangle. All the people who'd jumped up to cheer as the umpire called "Safe!" fell silent as the dust cleared. The A's runner lay writhing in pain, holding his leg.

"Robert looked at it," Garreth told Leara when she and Jenny had made their way to him through the crowd. "He doesn't think it's anything serious, but he recommended X rays, just to be safe. Chase's mother is too shaken up to drive him to the emergency room by herself.''

Leara grinned at Chase, who was seated on an ice chest with his injured leg supported on a cardboard box. She gave him the thumbs up sign when he bravely grinned back.

Garreth continued, ''Here are my car keys. If you wouldn't mind taking Jenny home with you, I could meet . . . *Jenny*? What happened?''

Garreth looked in amazement at his daughter, who stood next to Leara, very tired and rumpled and dirty, but smiling happily. He knelt and tweaked one of her curls, ''What happened to you? Did you slide home, too, like Chase?''

''No, Daddy. I got dirty when I played. I played with Georgie and Amelia and Freddie and Judy. We went under the bleachers—it's scary under there!''

He straightened, frowning. ''I guess Jenny slipped away from you. A four-year-old can be a handful.''

Disturbed by his tone, as if he was making excuses for her to cover a lapse, Leara said firmly, ''I knew exactly where she was at all times. She was playing with the other children—and having fun.''

Garreth's face darkened, his look incredulous. ''I can't believe you let her play under the bleachers, with all the filth under there!''

''When the kids went under, I shooed them back out. What's wrong?'' She could swear he was angry with her, but she couldn't see why.

''Mrs. Teagle takes her to the park every afternoon, and Jenny never comes home looking—''

''Mrs. Teagle—'' Leara began.

''Look, I have to go,'' he said. ''We'll talk later.''

FIVE

"Ssh!" Leara put her finger to her lips as she held the screen door for Garreth, then pointed to Jenny, who was hugging a fat pillow as she slept on the sofa. Her soiled clothes seemed even dirtier against the crisp white pillowcase.

"I think she enjoyed her day," Leara whispered as she caught Garreth's large hand in her small one and led the way into the kitchen.

Garreth smiled as he obediently followed. Leara had scraped her super-curly hair into a short ponytail on the crown of her head. Coppery tendrils too short to be captured were loose, curling around her face. She'd dusted her nose with powder, but the sprinkling of freckles there still showed through. In her cutoffs and striped T-shirt, she looked young; so much like the Leara he'd remembered . . . except for the way she filled that T-shirt, Garreth thought. In some ways, she had definitely matured.

"You haven't eaten, yet, have you?" she asked. Garreth shook his head, and Leara pointed him toward one of the two remaining kitchen chairs at the blue enameled table. He soon was enjoying a ham sandwich and a bowl of vegetable soup Leara had heated in the microwave.

Leara opened the ancient refrigerator and took out a pitcher of iced tea. "We went by Ferguson's and picked up the sandwiches from the deli section. While Jenny finished her lunch, I ran bath water, but when I came out of the bathroom, she'd crawled up on the couch and was sound asleep."

"I'm sorry. The emergency room took longer than I'd thought, and you ended up baby-sitting all day."

"Don't be sorry!" Leara said firmly. "Jenny and I enjoyed ourselves. In fact, we have a date for the park tomorrow—unless you have other plans for her?"

Garreth smiled, happy that Leara liked his daughter. Of course, he'd never doubted it—Lea was so warm and giving. That was something he'd always remembered whenever he'd thought about her through the years—to those who came within her sphere, she always gave wholeheartedly of herself, holding nothing back. And she was still giving, nurturing. Exactly as he'd thought of her through the years.

"Sounds nice," he said. "But I have a business meeting in the afternoon. It is the only time the investors could get together at the mall site," Garreth said regretfully.

"Who said you were invited?" Leara smiled mischievously as she filled two tumblers with iced tea. As she placed one of the glasses in front of him, he caught her hand and pulled her around to his side of the table, compelling her to sit down on his hard muscled thigh.

"Woman, every time I see you, I want to kiss you." He brushed coppery curls from her cheek, savoring the feel of her satin skin, the slight fragrance of jasmine that came from her hair.

Garreth's fingers on her skin made her shiver, though

they felt silky warm. Leara's eyelids drooped, her gray eyes darkening. Tracing his bottom lip with her finger, enjoying the firmness, the way it was slightly squared at the outer corners, she said huskily, "Then why don't you?"

"Because," Garreth said, nipping playfully at her finger, "I wanted to just spend time with you. Get to know you again. Talk—remember, taking it slowly . . ."

Whatever he would have said was lost in a small groan as Leara's playful fingers moved to his ear and she stroked the velvety inside whorl.

"You'd like to talk?" she whispered, then caught her breath sharply as Garreth slipped his hand underneath her shirt and cupped her full breast, his thumb unerringly finding her nipple through the thin fabric of her bra.

As he teased it into a taut peak, Garreth brushed her lips with light kisses, pulling back whenever she tried to deepen the contact. His mouth moved to the supple column of her throat, and Leara arched her back in pleasure. As she drank in his tangy male scent, she explored the taut muscles of his shoulders and combed her fingers through his silky, short hair, until he captured her hands and held them immobile.

"Oh! Yes, I like the way you talk, but does this have to be a one-sided conversation?" she gasped and Garreth chuckled. She tried to kiss him, but Garreth wouldn't take his lips from the sensitive curve where her neck joined her shoulder. When he moved the assault to her ear, she sighed.

Breaking free of his grasp, Leara captured his face between her palms and drew back so she could look into his eyes, her own a deep, smoky gray.

The look in the brown depths was warm and playful. He knew perfectly well how he was arousing her, yet frustrating her attempts to reciprocate.

"Enough," she admonished breathlessly, all too aware of the hard muscles beneath her rounded bottom and the male heat communicating itself to her from where her hips pressed the juncture of his thighs. "This won't be much of a conversation, unless you let me say something, too!"

She punctuated the sentence by kissing him deeply. When her tongue slipped between his teeth, tasting of warmth and promise, filling him with surging need, Garreth lost all thought of maintaining control. He thought of her bedroom, of the cool sheets and her warm body. Shifting Leara's weight, Garreth slipped his arm beneath her knees and rose.

Startled at suddenly being lifted, Leara flung out her arms, grasping for something solid, and knocked over his glass of iced tea.

"Oh no! Garreth, let me down!" Leara wriggled as the liquid ran off the edge of the table and drizzled on her clean linoleum.

"Damn!" Garreth muttered. He reluctantly set her on her feet and grabbed paper towels to help mop up the mess.

"Daddy? Daddy?" A sleepy Jenny, dragging her pillow, pushed open the swinging door between the kitchen and living room. "Daddy, I want Mr. Floppy."

Leara sighed with relief as she and Jenny entered the cooling shade of the trees that enclosed the park. The air felt heavy on her skin and smelled faintly of fresh-cut grass. Even the usually noisy birds seemed lulled into lethargy by the oppressive heat. The heat had wilted her spirit. Or, perhaps, it was the deep confusion in her heart and mind that was weighing her down.

Leara grasped Jenny's small hand in hers, and the little girl looked up at her with wide solemn eyes. She didn't respond to Leara's smile. Leara wondered why the child was so subdued. She had been like this ever since Garreth had dropped her off on his way to the meeting.

The investors, who had commissioned Garreth's firm to design a shopping mall, were in town to inspect the nearly completed facility. Garreth had asked Leara to go along, leaving Jenny in the care of the nanny. But Leara had promised Jenny an outing in the park.

Leara briefly closed her eyes, remembering the dark fires in Garreth's eyes as he'd pulled her into his arms for a brief, hard kiss before leaving for his meeting. That kiss had stirred her and left her wanting more—which had been exactly what he'd intended. The rat.

Now, she had to wonder if seeing her father kiss her was what had made Jenny subdued. The child was only a shadow of the little golden butterfly she'd been yesterday.

"Miss Leara," Jenny began.

"I like my friends to call me Leara."

"Leara, what're we gonna do?"

"What do you usually do when you come to the park?"

"Oh, sometimes I watch Mrs. Teagle do her knitting. It's fun to watch the needles poke in and out of the yarn, almost like they're dancing." Her little fingers danced themselves as she demonstrated. "Sometimes I play with a doll or read a book."

"Read a book?"

"Well, not really." Jenny's mouth gave a little quirk as she confessed, "I can only read a little, so I make up stories to go with the pictures in my books."

The recreation of a lonely child, Leara thought. "Mrs. Teagle reads to you, doesn't she?"

"At bedtime. She reads three pages every night." Jenny held up three fingers and counted them off, "One, two, three."

Leara's eyes widened in disbelief, then she gave a small shake of her head. Three pages. Every night. After generously allowing Jenny to sit on a park bench and watch knitting. Leara decided that she'd like to meet this woman, Teagle!

"Would you like to meet some new friends?" Leara asked after gaining control of her tongue and refusing it permission to say what she thought of Mrs. Teagle. Several young preschoolers were playing on the swings, looking totally oblivious to the heat.

Jenny's eyes became instantly shy. "I don't know."

"But, didn't you enjoy playing with the others at the baseball game?" By this time they had reached a cluster of benches under a huge oak tree, and Leara sat down, pulling Jenny around to face her. For the first time since Jenny had watched her father's car pull away from the house, Leara saw the glimmer of a smile.

"Yes, we had lots of fun." The slight lift at the corners of Jenny's mouth that had given Leara hope that she was getting through was suddenly gone.

"What's the matter, Jenny?" Leara asked gently. "Did someone do something yesterday that bothered you? You liked all the other kids, didn't you?"

"Oh, yes!" There was finally a hint of enthusiasm in Jenny's manner. Her eyes lighted her whole face. "Especially Amelia. She was so much fun!" Jenny suddenly seemed like a butterfly about to take flight, poised on her toes, almost bouncing in her joy. Then the glow faded as the truth emerged, "But Mrs. Teagle was cross with me last night for getting so very dirty." Jenny sat on the bench and brushed invisible dust from her immaculate bright red shorts set. "And she said my hair was so knotted from the tangles . . . she pulled my hair when she brushed it. It hurt." The bright little eyes found Leara's face as Jenny explained, "I have to be good and stay clean. Mrs. Teagle says that's what my daddy wants, a sweet little girl who stays clean and behaves like a lady.''

It was obvious to Leara that what Jenny wanted most was to be what her daddy wanted. *How dare she!* A wave of rage swept through Leara at the emotional blackmail the nanny had used on this child. A child had the right to be a child for the few short years that the world allowed it. More than that, it was necessary in order to have a happy, well-balanced adult life. This Teagle woman had manipulated Jenny by implying that her father wouldn't love her unless she was perfect— the unfeeling harpy!

Leara had seen so-called child care professionals use similar tactics before, and it was usually because cleaning up after a perfect little doll was much less work than the mess generated by a normal, active four-year-old.

This Teagle should be making Jenny's world safe for Jenny to explore; encouraging her absorbent curiosity and innate creativity. Instead, this prim and proper little girl next to her was being forced into an adult mold. Didn't Garreth see what was happening?

"My darling Jenny, did you know that you can have fun and still stay clean and neat?'' Leara said brightly, unwilling to again make Jenny prey to Mrs. Teagle's manipulations. "And you must meet my friend.'' Leara reached into her voluminous skirt pocket and pulled out a bright orange tennis ball on which a pair of eyes and a large smiling mouth had been inscribed. "His name is Hairy, because he's fuzzy all over. He loves to play.''

Jenny took the proffered ball, looked straight into the black-dot eyes, and said, "Hello, Hairy, I'm Jenny. Would you like to play with me?'' She nodded to the ball as though it was answering her, and Leara silently congratulated herself on her choice.

Years ago, when she had begun working in the day

care center, she had sewed the full skirts with the kangaroo pockets for this very purpose; a place to hide all the small, wonderful toys of childhood. Now, the smiling orange ball helped an imaginative child learn to play.

"Throw him to me, Jenny." Leara ran a short distance away and held her hands out in front of her, encouraging Jenny to get up and toss the ball. Jenny threw the ball wildly off target. Leara laughed and ran after it. After a long moment's hesitation, Jenny followed, her blond curls bouncing. When Leara caught up ball, she tossed it gently in Jenny's direction. "Here he comes, Jenny! Tell him what you want him to do!"

"Come here, Hairy! Come here!" The orange face bounced on the ground twice, and Jenny held out her hands, turning her face aside and closing her eyes tightly as the ball bounced straight at her. It bounced against her chest and plopped right into her hands.

The shocked, delighted expression on Jenny's face sent Leara into peals of laughter. And just as suddenly, the child joined her mirth, her tiny tinkling laugh reminding Leara of sunlight sparkles on water.

"Can I play?" A timid voice spoke from behind Leara. Jenny peeked around Leara at the child. When Leara turned, she saw a boy of about five, his cropped red hair spiked on top of his head and a pair of golden eyes almost lost amid a face full of freckles of the same color.

Leara stooped down to be on eye level with the boy. "And what is your name?" she asked.

Hand in his mouth, the golden eyes wide, the little boy hung back, suddenly frightened. Jenny stepped forward and held up the orange ball. In a squeaky voice, she said, "My name is Hairy 'cause I'm fuzzy. What's your name?" as she nodded the ball.

The little boy hid his mouth with his hand and giggled. "Bobby," he said, so softly that Leara barely heard him. She sat very still, afraid to disturb the magic that was happening to Jenny. The lonely girl was reaching out.

"Hi, Bobby. I'm Jenny. Me and Leara and Hairy were playing catch. Can you catch?"

"Sure I can!"

"Good." Jenny nodded and handed Leara the ball. "Can we throw Hairy to Bobby, too, Leara?"

"Of course," Leara agreed. "But first, Bobby, ask your mother if it's okay." Leara did not encourage small children to trust strangers—and she was a stranger to Bobby. She encouraged them to trust their parents' opinion of a situation.

He ran back, nodding. Soon the children were enjoying a hectic game of catch, with many dropped balls. Other children soon joined in, and much of the afternoon had slipped away before Leara realized it.

As she was sitting on the bench catching her breath, her mind kept going back to Garreth and his relationship with his daughter. Leara didn't doubt that he loved Jenny wholeheartedly. But she also knew that it was difficult being a single parent. He had probably taken the crisp, neat child the Teagle woman kept before him as a sign that she was doing a good job.

Leara decided that she had to talk to him about Jenny; to try to open his eyes to his daughter's needs. Garreth was so tender and caring, he would see her point.

Her thoughts turned to her renewed relationship with Garreth, and she wondered where it was going. He was damned attractive—maturity had only made him sexier. But, what if they found that's all this thing between them was—just sexual attraction flavored heavily with nostalgia?

"Hello, Leara."

Garreth! Leara thought. But, when she turned, her face full of joy, it wasn't Garreth. It was Quint.

"Hello, Quint." Her expression reflected the roller coaster drop from the top of the world back down to earth. "What brings you here?"

Quint didn't seem to notice as he sat beside her on the bench. "I was driving by and I saw you out there with those kids. I couldn't resist stopping to watch." His eyes took in her tousled hair and slightly flushed face, the airy cotton blouse and skirt. She looked barely older than her charges. "You're very good with them, Leara. Is that why you like to work in day care? Because you're still a child in your heart?" His voice was gentle, caressing.

Leara was surprised and a little suspicious at this kinder, gentler version of the man she knew too well. "How's the dealership doing?" she asked, to put the conversation on a less personal level.

He brightened. "We broke the sales record for Midwest dealers last month. I never expected to be doing so well this soon."

This was new, too. The usual swagger wasn't there. All she saw was boyish enthusiasm. "That's terrific. I always said if you put out the effort you could do anything." She looked at him, seeing the expensive watch, the well-cut suit, the startling blue eyes. He had always been good-looking, but success, and this newfound maturity, gave him an added attractiveness. She felt a tiny stab of regret. She had married him for the wrong reasons; used him to escape from Columbus. She'd tried to make it up to him by being a good wife, but it just hadn't worked. At least Quint seemed to be—at last— accepting their breakup. Maybe now he'd find someone who was right for him.

"How's everything with you? Have you finished here

yet? I thought you'd have gone home by now," he said.

"Oh, Becky can manage without me a few days. I'm not totally indispensable." She smiled. "But, I will be going back tonight. I miss the kids." She glanced over to where Jenny and her friends were engaged in a frantic game of tag.

"Yeah. You always had a knack with kids." His eyes found and held hers. "You know, I was jealous when you started doing so well with the day care. I thought you were trying to show me up. I had such trouble keeping a job, and you made it look so easy. I was too stupid to see that the reason you made it work was that you gave it all you had."

Leara took stock again. This man certainly seemed different from the childish, self-centered Quint she had divorced.

Suddenly, Jenny and Bobby raced up to the bench. Eyeing Quint with distrust, Jenny said, "Miss . . . I mean, Leara, Hairy got caught in a tree!" She turned and pointed at a tall poplar. The bright orange ball was wedged in the fork of two limbs about ten feet off the ground.

"I can take care of that. Leave it to me," Quint assured Jenny. Within a few minutes, Quint had climbed up and dropped Hairy into Jenny's waiting hands.

"Thanks, sir. My friend Hairy would've been lonely up there," she told him after he'd dropped the last few feet to the ground.

Leara marveled as he went down on one knee and touched the little girl on the cheek. "Princess, if he's your friend, he's a very lucky guy."

Jenny reached out and patted him back, as though it was just the right thing to do. "You can be my friend, too, if you want."

For just a moment, Leara thought she saw Quint's eyes mist. But then it was gone. His electric blue eyes followed Jenny as she ran back to the other kids with the ball, then he turned to her with a rueful smile.

"You know, Leara, what the little girl said about friends hit me hard. See, I lost my best friend a while back, and I'd really like to see you again—just as friends. I know we—I—made a mess of things in the past by demanding more than you could give, and it wasn't your fault you couldn't give it. You were always up front with me. I knew that you'd married me on the rebound. But, for all those years that we were married, your friendship was there for me. Whenever I was uncertain, or disappointed, or just needed someone to talk to, you were always there. You were always my best friend. And it's been tough being without my best friend. I'd like us to be friends again."

Looking into his eyes, she felt a familiar prick of guilt for having ever married him. Quint had been willing to accept her on any terms, and she had taken advantage of that. It had been a totally selfish act, a way to escape her father's domination, because she didn't have the strength of character to deal with it on her own. Now, she was acutely conscious that she could never make it up to Quint.

"Sure. If you ever need someone to talk to, I wouldn't mind a call."

"Will you be here for the reunion next weekend? I guess you and Conroe have already made plans to go?"

"It's been mentioned," she said, being deliberately vague. Actually, she and Garreth had made no plans yet.

"Will you promise me a dance?" he asked.

"If I see you there."

Just then, Jenny came running back to them. "Are you leaving?"

"Yup. I have to get back to work. Lots of cars to sell." Turning to Leara, he said, "We're having our monthly Sunday Madness sale. All prices slashed to the bone!" he said in a mock announcer's voice. "Fortunately, buyers don't realize that cars have very few bones." He grinned and winked at Leara.

"Thank you again, sir." Jenny held out her hand and Quint bent over and solemnly shook it.

"Tell all your friends good-bye for me, will you, Princess?"

"Yes, sir. Bye!" And she was off running to the others.

Quint straightened and, after a quick sidelong glance at Leara to see that he had her attention, looked thoughtfully after the little blond girl. "You know, Leara, there have been times lately when I've wished I hadn't been so adamant about not having kids. It might be nice to have a little face like that one around." He turned toward a stunned Leara and reached up and caressed her cheek. "I'd better be getting back. You take care." He was gone before Leara could speak.

She hadn't seen the tall figure standing in the shade of the trees on the other side of the park, watching, or the sly smile that had curved Quint's lips when he'd realized that Garreth Conroe had seen him and Leara together. This afternoon had gone even better than he'd planned.

_____ SIX _____

The sun was touching the horizon as Garreth drove the car along the streets of Columbus. Leara glanced at Jenny, who sat in the back seat playing quietly with the finger puppets Leara had produced from her copious pocket and given to the child.

"She's very good at entertaining herself, isn't she?" Leara asked, trying to broach the subject of Jenny's environment. Leara was determined to make Garreth aware of the child's need for more spontaneity and interaction with other children, and less Teagle-ism.

"Yes. She has a great imagination," Garreth said, barely glancing at Leara when he spoke.

Ever since he'd picked them up in the park before taking them for pizza, Garreth had been polite. Distant.

At first, Leara had assumed his meeting hadn't gone well. Now, she was at a loss. She stared at his profile and ached inside to reach out and caress the square line of his jaw, to feel the slight roughness of the whiskers just beneath the skin. The tangy male scent of him invited her to unfasten her seat belt and slide close to

79

him, to rest her head on his shoulder in the circle of his arm.

The cool reserve he'd shown toward her all afternoon kept her firmly on her side of the car. Why was he so determinedly unapproachable? *Have* I done something?

At least Jenny seemed oblivious to the tension between the adults. The child had talked brightly between bites of pizza about the fun she'd had in the park, and Garreth had encouraged her, drawing her out. But whenever Leara had entered the conversation, he'd answered her questions succinctly. And when Leara's puzzled gray eyes had met his brown ones, she'd seen accusation in them. Was it because Jenny had been running and playing with other children when he'd come to pick them up? That would be utterly ridiculous!

After she tried to pierce his reserve several times, Leara's own anger had flared and she had matched his cool tone and impersonal comments. But Garreth's attitude hurt. Could this be the man who'd told her that he'd never found anything close to what they'd once shared? Was this the same man who'd wanted to renew their relationship the moment he'd discovered that she was free? was this the man who'd held her in his arms just yesterday and left her head spinning this afternoon from the promise in his kiss?

Leara unconsciously shook her head, unable to sort out his sudden change in attitude; unable to understand how this change of heart hurt her when they'd found each other again only a few days ago. She was glad she was driving back to Gary tonight. She needed distance between them; time to sort out her feelings. Apparently Garreth did, too.

Leara had promised herself that before she left town, she'd make him aware of Jenny's needs. Unfortunately, this granite profile he presented wasn't making it any easier for her to tell him that he was missing something vital when it came to his young daughter.

Leara gave up for the moment and stared out her window as Garreth pulled up before a comfortably large home in one of the more select sections of town.

"Would you like to come in for a drink while I tuck Jenny into bed?" he asked Leara as he slid out of the car. His tone was polite. Impersonal.

"I not sleep—" Jenny hid a yawn behind a pair of bunnies, which perched on her fingers.

"Of course you aren't," the large man smiled as he ducked his head in the back door, unfastening his daughter's safety belt.

"I'll wait here," Leara said.

"I won't be long."

As Garreth lifted Jenny out of the car, she suddenly demanded to kiss Leara good night. Smiling, Leara got out and went around the car to receive a hug and a wet kiss. She watched wistfully as Garreth turned and took his daughter inside.

When he returned, she said, "I need to talk to you about something before I drive back home tonight."

"Fine." The one word was glacial. Garreth's face was a cold mask as he started the car and pulled away from the curb. "You're driving back alone?" The dark edge to his question was unmistakable.

He mentally braced himself for her answer. In his mind, he still saw Quint and Leara together in the park, Quint's hand touching her soft cheek, the smile that had graced her face as she looked up at him.

Damn! In his joy at having found her again, Garreth had pushed Quint from his mind, never considered the possibility that she and Quint might reconcile.

"What's that supposed to mean?"

"Nothing."

His fist clenched around the steering wheel as he

remembered Leara's face turned up to his, flushed with desire, her eyes dark and smoky with passion. She had been married to Quint for eight years—had she looked at Quint like that when he'd kissed her? Made love to her? Did Quint still affect her that way?

Was she going to choose Quint again?

Leara stared at Garreth. The tight, clipped word was like his expression, sharp with anger.

"In the park, you saw Quint talking to me, didn't you?" Leara said in sudden understanding. "You're jealous!"

Garreth didn't answer immediately. His face in the soft light suddenly looked young, vulnerable.

"Yes. I am jealous. Damned jealous! I keep remembering his hand touching your cheek . . ."

"And . . . ?" Leara prompted gently.

Garreth glanced at her again. "And when did you get so damned perceptive?" he asked.

"Quint found me in the park. I didn't invite him to be there. But that's not all that's bothering you, is it?" she asked with a small, sad smile.

"He touched your cheek. And you let him. It made me remember that you were married to him for eight years—"

"Garreth, it was only a friendly gesture." Leara's voice was soft, but it offered no apology.

She hadn't done anything to apologize for.

Garreth suddenly felt ashamed of his behavior. He had made the whole evening uncomfortable just because he was insecure. And jealous. The sight of quint Lockwood touching Leara took him painfully back to those high school days when Lockwood had done his damnedest to take Leara away. And Lockwood had succeeded.

But you were responsible, Conroe! Hadn't he pushed her right into Lockwood's arms? Was he going to make that mistake again?

Garreth reached out and gently grasped Leara's shoulder. The warmth of his palm through her blouse seared her like a flame. Impulsively, she slid across the seat until his arm was around her, and his warm body was snugly pressed against her own. She felt his sigh and the bunched muscles in his arm relax. His hand curled protectively around her arm.

"I am jealous, Lea," he said simply. "Where Lockwood is concerned, don't expect me to be rational." He paused, then asked huskily, "Do you have to go back tonight?"

Leara closed her eyes as she realized what he was really asking—if she would spend the night with him. She snuggled into his warmth, drinking in the male scent of him, the faint spice of his cologne, but shook her head. "I do. But we could drive around for a while." She was unwilling to relinquish his nearness just yet, but she was equally unwilling to allow him any closer.

"Sure. There's something I'd like you to see, anyway." Garreth's words were as soft and gentle as his touch as he stroked her hair. She heard his pulse throbbing under her ear as she rested her head on his shoulder. He could take her anywhere, as long as they remained in the safety of the car, where she could keep the overwhelming passion at bay and enjoy this comfortable intimacy.

Garreth took a turn into an older neighborhood, where small wood-framed houses huddled close together along friendly tree-lined streets. "This project is special to me, Lea. This neighborhood is on a downward spiral. The houses are old, rundown. The wiring is outdated and the insulation is practically nonexistent. More and more have become vacant; eventually they would be torn down and the area would be rezoned commercial."

"These cottages could be charming. All they need—"

"All they need is a ton of work, which we're putting into them. Look at these places." On the next block was a row of houses in varying stages of renovation. Soft-colored vinyl siding, contrasting shutters, and modern, insulated windows made these houses much more attractive than their counterparts in the previous block. The signs in the front yards read, "Conroe, Gordon and Associates, Ltd."

"Marijo?" Leara was stunned. M.J. had never mentioned that she and Garreth were partners in any projects.

"Yes. It's her brainchild, actually," he said modestly. "The target market is young couples struggling to own their own homes. I think it's a worthwhile project, even though the profit margin is very small."

As he drove slowly, Leara noticed that every third or fourth house had been, or was being, torn down. "What happened to the houses in between?" she asked. "Weren't they repairable?"

"The houses in the poorest conditions are being torn down to make space for communal play areas—like small parks."

Leara watched Garreth's face as he pointed out the special adornments to each house. It was obvious he believed strongly in what he and Marijo were doing. This person was more like the Garreth she had known years ago. He'd had dreams of building wonderful homes for families to live and love in. It pleased her to think that he hadn't lost track of those dreams.

"I'm impressed," she said, smiling up at him.

"Thank you." Garreth smiled, his voice husky. "I guess I'd better get you back."

He began to speed up as they drove out of the area where the renovations were being done. On the corner, Leara spotted a large, weather-beaten Victorian house with a FOR SALE sign staked in the huge tree-filled yard. "Stop!" She caught his arm.

Garreth brought the car to a halt at the curb, and Leara hopped out. The setting sun turned the sky to brilliant coral, contrasting with the faded blue of the house. She took in the beautiful styling of the old building, with its peeling white-painted gingerbread trim, huge porch, and widow's walk. It was three stories high, with tall windows everywhere to let in plenty of light. The double front door was set with oval glass. And even though the dark uncurtained windows made it obvious that the place was empty, it seemed to beckon to Leara. It must have been a showplace in its day.

Her mind was suddenly full of images of the house—not as it stood now, empty and forlorn, but bright with color. And surrounded by playing children. She could see the rooms painted in soft pastels, filled with small furniture and laughing faces. It was as though this place was a magical house built just for kids.

"What a mausoleum." Garreth's comment wasn't as scathing in tone as the words implied. He stood beside her shaking his head.

"But, it's beautiful!" Leara exclaimed. "It would be a wonderful place for children!"

"Yes, it is beautiful. But who has a family big enough to fill it, even if they could afford it?" He pointed to the roof, which, even in the fading light of the sunset, showed dips and missing shingles. "The roof would have to be redone, and even if it was in good repair, the heating bill would be astronomical."

Leara grimaced at his practicality. He was tearing apart a dream, which had suddenly popped into her head. This house could be a wonderful day care center. A magic castle . . . A dream that could bring her back to Columbus.

She turned and let Garreth help her back into the car.

When he brought her home, Garreth's good-bye kiss was long and deep. It threatened to overpower her resolve to put some distance between them, to give them both time to think. It took all her strength to push herself away from him and slip through the door. She wistfully watched him walk to his car. He had managed to garner her promise to return next weekend for the reunion. To her surprise, she found herself looking forward to it.

Leara was on her way to Gary before she remembered that she hadn't talked to him about Jenny and Mrs. Teagle.

The smell of barbecue smoke and the sounds of children playing and adults laughing permeated the air of the large park. As Leara made her way toward the picnic table where Marijo was busily setting out containers of food, people called out greetings to her. Smiling, she waved and called back, sometimes turning a questioning look to Garreth and whispering, "Who is that?"

Mostly, Garreth, who trailed along behind her, laden with lounge chairs and a large cooler containing soft drinks and a bowl of macaroni salad, could only shake his head.

"Daddy, Daddy! Kimmi says I can stay with her and play. Can I, Daddy?" Jenny rushed up to them and danced up and down in her eagerness. M.J. had taken charge of Jenny when Leara and Garreth had stopped by on their way to the picnic.

"Yes, she's already informed me that she's going to be your sitter for the picnic." Garreth smiled at his daughter as she ran off, her feet hardly touching the ground.

Leara suspected that Kimmi's interest had been inspired by Marijo, to whom Leara had poured out her feelings about the quality of care Garreth's daughter was getting.

"Hey! Conroe!" a large man in cutoff jean shorts called from a group of men tossing a football. "You up for a game of touch football? We need a couple more players."

Garreth grinned back at the man and shrugged, since that was all he could do, loaded down as he was.

"Is that Chet Parker?" Leara asked as she began to relieve Garreth of his many burdens.

"Sure is." Marijo's eyes were sparkling with mirth. "He's become quite the ladies' man since high school. He was named as corespondent in two divorce cases that I know of."

"You're kidding!" leara stared at Chet. He was getting an early start on middle-aged spread. His belly hung a good six inches over his waistband and revealed a love of beer. His hairline had receded all the way to his crown, but he'd let the fringe grow and wore it pulled back in a short ponytail. "I wonder what his secret is," she mused as she unloaded the shopping bag of paper plates and cups.

"I understand he's quite romantic," Marijo mock-whispered to her. "In fact, I've been considering availing myself of his services." Smirking, she cast a sideways glance at her husband.

"The hell you are, woman!" Bill boomed, falling into the game. "I'll see you tied to the bed first!"

"Oooo. My hero!" Marijo squealed, throwing her arms around Bill's neck in a fake swoon. "Is that a promise?"

Leara smiled fondly. The two of them hadn't changed in all the years she'd known them. They still looked at one another like two teenagers in love.

She felt a pang of regret that she and Garreth hadn't had the love and joy over the last ten years that could have been theirs. And, despite the physical attraction she felt, she wondered if they could ever have the kind of relationship her best friend had been blessed with.

"C'mon, Garreth. Let's leave the women to their gossip and get to that football. I feel like tackling Chet in a very vulnerable area."

"Remember your bad knee!" M.J. called after him and added something in rapid Spanish that made her husband of ten years blush.

Laughing, Leara turned to Garreth, and her laughter died as she was captured and drawn into a pair of sherry brown eyes. Garreth's lips drooped and his eyes darkened as his gaze moved to her lips.

He watched in fascination, oblivious to all around him, as Laura's lips parted and her small pink tongue darted out to moisten them. He felt a bolt of heat surge through him at the sight.

As he'd walked behind her earlier, he'd been mesmerized by the way her shorts hugged her neatly rounded bottom and showed a long expanse of leg that belied her height. Now, he noticed that her satin skin was glowing with a fine sheen of perspiration. The loose crinkle-cotton shirt became semitransparent with the sun behind her, and he could see the outline of her lacy white bra against her skin. The outline became more pronounced as she raised her arms, lifting her coppery curls to let the cooling breeze slip down her collar. And the heat, which was growing in his loins, became an ache.

I could scoop her up and carry her somewhere, Garreth thought. Somewhere very private. Somewhere he could satisfy this need to possess her, to make love to her, slowly and tenderly—or maybe not so tenderly.

In all their years apart, he'd never made love to a woman who'd affected him as deeply as Leara had—and they'd both been green kids then, fumbling and inexperienced. He had to find out if that special magic that had haunted him all these years would still be there between them when they were in each other's arms.

And if it wasn't?

And if this thing he was feeling was only nostalgia, as Leara had suggested from the start? What if they had both changed too much to pick up the pieces? They'd been apart so long. . . .

Garreth refused to consider that possibility. Catching her slender waist, he pulled her to him and captured her mouth in a brief, hard kiss. "A kiss for luck, remember?" Garreth said. She had always kissed him before a game. He didn't release her immediately; he was enjoying the way her soft curves fit so neatly against his own hard frame.

"Are you playing, Conroe?" Bill called, and Leara stepped away, her breathing uneven.

Something primitive and male was in Garreth's smile as he trotted over to where the men were choosing up sides. He was powerless against this aching desire for her that gripped him whenever he was near her, but at least he'd reassured himself that she felt the same way. On the phone during the week, Leara had talked again of their need to go slowly, to be sure of what they wanted. Garreth only knew that if he had to wait much longer to feel her naked against him, to feel her soft flesh tighten around him as he slowly sheathed himself in her . . .

Take it slowly, hell! He was ready to explode with frustration!

He couldn't know that Leara had done a hundred and eighty degree turn in her thinking since that conversation. She had decided that the best way to get in touch with what they were really feeling underneath all the chemistry was to end the sexual tension between them.

And she intended to do just that. Tonight.

As Leara watched the football game, a wry smile curved her mouth as she realized that getting their "real feelings" out did not concern her half as much at this moment as her desire to get Garreth into bed. Now, he had stripped off his shirt—he was quarterback of the "skins team"—and his tightly muscled chest and arms rippled with his movements. The hair on his chest, thicker than she remembered, sparkled with little sun-kissed diamonds of sweat where it trailed down into the waistband of his shorts. His brown legs looked power-ful, though he was trim rather than bulky.

As Garreth back-pedaled, faked the handoff, then turned and passed the football, the muscles in his shoul-ders delineated themselves beneath his sweat-slicked skin and a frisson danced along Leara's nerve endings at the thought of being held in those arms in just a few short hours.

He looked almost fierce with his concentration on the game. She remembered his look of hunger a few min-utes earlier. When he glanced toward her while walking back to the scrimmage line after a play, she saw it again. There was a ferocity in that look that promised he wouldn't wait much longer.

She didn't want him to. Tonight, she told him si-lently. Tonight we'll get past this incredible chemistry and find out if there is anything underneath it.

But what if they found out that's all there was— physical attraction and echoes of a past romance? And, even if the feelings of love were really still there after all these years, could they really recapture the past?

"Looks like Conroe's side is winning," Quint said, coming up behind her.

Blushing, Leara turned her attention back to the table of food and started opening bags of potato chips. Strug-gling to relax her passion-tight throat, she said lightly, "He always was good at sports."

"Yeah, I guess he was. I might have given him a run for his money if I'd played."

"You never liked football, anyway. Track was always your sport." She was trying to get the subject onto anything but Garreth. She had no intention of discussing Garreth with Quint. She looked at the people around the other tables for the missing Marijo. "Where's your date?" she asked when she couldn't spot M.J.

Quint shrugged. "She had something to do this afternoon. I think maybe she's getting her hair done for the dance tonight."

"Marijo told me she works at Castle's Restaurant. Is that where you met her?" She wasn't really curious about the woman, but she wanted to keep the talk light. What she really wanted was for Quint to just go away. She was suddenly uncomfortable because he was so near—she could swear she felt Garreth's eyes on them!

A feeling of déjà vu swept over her. How many times as she'd watched Garreth at football practice had Quint sat down beside her, uninvited? How many times had Garreth seen them together and later cornered Quint, the two of them wanting to tear each other apart? And how many times had she intervened, promising that she'd never again speak to the one who threw the first punch?

Quint straddled the bench, facing her, ignoring her silent message to leave. "She's a waitress there. Her name is Fran Carlton. You'll meet her tonight." He leaned toward her a little, smiling inwardly as he thought about Leara's questioning M.J. about him. That meant she still felt something! He'd known that his success was all it would take—that and a little time to gloss over some of his past mistakes.

He smiled again. "You are coming, aren't you? I'm looking forward to having that dance with you. Just for old-times' sake." His smile grew wistful.

"Yes. I suppose I can save you a dance."

"Great! We always were fire on the dance floor," he said, leaning back and holding out his arms as though he held a partner. "I hope it won't be our last dance. I meant what I said about staying friends. Hey, if you're staying at your grandmother's, it wouldn't be out of the way for me to pick you up."

"How about Fran?" Leara asked.

"Don't get me wrong—Fran's a great kid, but—"

"I'm staying at the hotel," Leara said quietly. "I'm going with Garreth."

His smile faltered a little, and an expression she couldn't define slipped across his face.

"So you and Conroe have picked up where you left off." It wasn't a question. "I guess I always knew you two would find each other again." He said it lightly, but there was an undercurrent in his voice that disturbed her.

"We . . . we just started seeing each other. It's not what everybody seems to think." *Not yet,* she added silently.

"Really? Does that mean I still have a chance to change your mind?" His tone was light and teasing, as was the easy grin on his face.

"You mean about being friends?" She turned the question back on him, knowing that was not what he meant. So, the leopard hadn't really changed his spots, after all. He'd just covered them up.

"Or something," he said. Looking back toward the group on the playing field, he stood up. "Maybe I'll see if I can go spell somebody. I think I can still remember how to play." He mimicked throwing a pass. "See you later, Lea. Be sure and save me that dance."

The ball game broke up a short time later as the voice of the former principal came over loudspeakers atop a makeshift bandstand. After speeches and recognition of those classmates who had gone on to do special things, the organized games began.

Leara watched in amazement as Garreth and Jenny took the blue ribbon in the egg race. She laughed out loud at the intense expression on Jenny's face as she concentrated all her effort on keeping the boiled egg in the spoon. Jenny hopped up and down at the sidelines while her daddy made the return trip, his strides level and long.

During the men's sack race, Quint renewed the rivalry he'd started during the football game. When the contestants lined up at the starting line, jostling for position, Quint and Garreth were next to each other, exchanging glares more suited to two gladiators about to fight to the death, not hop to the finish.

This is ridiculous! Leara thought. *Utterly, childishly ridiculous!* Before the men had made it halfway to the finish line, Quint had crossed into Garreth's path and was trying, successfully, to slow Garreth's progress. As a result, both lost the race.

The other games went the same way, with Garreth and Quint going head to head, like two Olympic decathletes. When he and Quint went head on, each captaining a different volleyball team in the semifinals, Leara marched in and took Garreth firmly by the arm.

"Come and eat. Marijo is muttering in Spanish about her ribs drying up like beef jerky as she tries to keep them warm for you."

But Garreth was not to be deterred. "I'll be there as soon as we win," he said and, before she could react, bent her backward in a deep, searching kiss. "For luck, again," Garreth grinned as he released her.

When Leara's head stopped spinning with the effects, she saw Quint watching her, his face solemn, and realized the kiss had been for Quint's benefit—as did most of the people present from the sudden quiet that possessed the spectators. Most everyone remembered Garreth's and Quint's old rivalry over her and knew, also, that she'd been married to Quint. To Leara's embarrassment, she felt like a stuffed animal prize at a carnival.

Leara angrily made her way back to the picnic table. "Those two are carrying on like they belong in elementary school! If this keeps up. I'm going back to Gary—before lunch!"

"These are great ribs," Garreth commented later, when the contest was over and his team had walked away with the ribbon.

"The macaroni salad isn't bad, either," Bill prompted, tilting his head in Leara's direction and signaling Garreth with his eyes.

Leara hadn't said a word to Garreth since his little performance during the games. But the air was full of unspoken words and a tension that wasn't entirely angry.

SEVEN

Garreth heard the sound of the elevator doors opening, turned toward them, and froze as a vision in peach silk floated out. He forgot the apology he was going to offer for his juvenile behavior during the games that afternoon; he forgot the speech he'd rehearsed that had been intended to make her quit her baby-sitting job in Gary and move in with him.

Leara's off-the-shoulder dress was a frilly confection, with wide ruffles of lace gathered at the low neckline and hem. The full skirt made her waist look tiny enough to span with his hands, and its short length showed off her shapely tanned legs. Her shining copper curls were pulled back from her face by flowered combs that sparkled like her silvery eyes—had he ever noticed before how long her lashes were?

Heads turned as she moved to him, and he felt a surge of pride at the thought that she was here with him.

"You look wonderful tonight, Lea. Like Cinderella," Garreth murmured. He was pleased to see a slight blush redden her cheeks at his subtle reminder of the first time they'd gone to a formal affair, her senior prom, and the first time they'd made love.

"Thank you." Leara's words came out as a husky purr. His use of her pet name, and the seductive tone of his voice, made her throat tight with emotion. Smiling a secret smile, she tore her eyes away from his warm, brown gaze and looked around the ballroom as they entered it.

Garreth didn't know that she had planned for this night to be the realization of a fantasy. On the day she found this dress that was driving Garreth to distraction, she had gone to a lingerie shop and found something even more wonderful for later.

Yes, she had very definite plans for tonight. But if Garreth kept this up, she wondered just who would be seducing whom.

Garreth circled Leara's waist with his arm, pulling her against his side as they made their way through the crowd to the table where M.J. and Bill sat. The heat of her skin through the thin silk at her waist warmed his hand. He savored the faint, delicate fragrance of her perfume. It was like white flowers, soft and intoxicating.

"The decorations are wonderful," Leara said, looking at the bands of deep blue netting with bright spangles draped from the ceiling and the walls. Tiny white lights winked amid the gathers of net. Gilded silver stars hung in clusters from the midnight "sky" represented by the fabric, and a silver mirrored ball ten feet in diameter hung in the center of the room, like a full moon. Beneath it, a statue of a woman was poised on a stone in the middle of a miniature pool, a tipped vase balanced on her shoulder. From the vase, a never ending stream of water cascaded into the pool, which was complete with lily pads. "Oh, Garreth, it's Starlight and Moonshine—the theme from the prom!"

As Garreth held her chair for her, Marijo said, "Denise Greene planned everything. She's an interior designer in Indianapolis now. You remember her, don't you? She was the tallest girl in homeroom and flat as a washboard. She didn't have a date for the prom and didn't go. That's her over by the punch bowl."

"If she was flat as a board, she's certainly changed," Bill said appreciatively as he eyed the slinky brunette's enticing curves. His breath came out in a whoosh as Marijo's elbow found the soft part of his stomach.

"As I was saying," M.J. said, glaring at her husband in mock ferocity, "poor thing didn't have a date and stayed home, so she's gone to a lot of trouble to re-create our prom so that she can enjoy it now. I guess we all have our fantasies."

Bill said, irrepressibly, "I bet Denise didn't have any trouble getting a date this time around. Boy, has she changed. Don't elbow me again, woman! I'll be forced to file suit for husband abuse."

As the band struck up a slow song, which had been popular ten years before, Garreth took Leara's hand. "Want to dance?" She nodded. Rising, Garreth said to Bill and M.J., "Excuse us. I don't want to be called as a witness against my own business partner." He winked at M.J.

Leara let Garreth lead her onto the dance floor and placed her head on his shoulder as he circled her with his arms and began leading her to the soft strains of the music. The tiny lights sparkling overhead added to her feeling of unreality, of being in a magical world of soft silk and strong arms; of the musk and spice that was Garreth's own individual scent mixed with his cologne; of his breath against her cheek as he whispered her name.

Magic. She could feel it; this night was magic, just like her prom night had been ten years before. She was in Garreth's arms again—magic! Everything had come full circle. . . .

"May I cut in?" a male voice asked.

Leara gasped and turned in Garreth's tense arms.

"Get lost, Lockwood." Garreth's words were a growl. "Leara's with me."

Quint, who was resplendent in his black tuxedo, assumed an injured expression. "Is that why Leara's promised to save a dance for me?" Then to Leara, "And, this was our song—remember, Lea? We danced to it on our wedding night. We set my old radio up on the table in that motel room. . . ."

Leara caught Garreth's hands as they curled into fists. She stamped her foot. "I won't have this!"

Neither man paid attention. Looking from Garreth to Quint, at the violent intent in both men's eyes, she felt as powerless as she'd felt ten years before.

Quint had tried to cut in while she'd been dancing with Garreth at her senior prom, and Garreth and Quint had come to blows. Garreth's fist had split Quint's lip before the chaperons could separate the two, and she and Garreth had been asked to leave.

Well, she wouldn't have it! Not this time!

She tugged forcefully on Garreth's lapels until he reluctantly took his gaze from Quint and looked at her. Leara was glowering. "I'd like some champagne, please. Now. This is a party."

Garreth's face was dark as he read the silent message in her eyes—Don't spoil everyone's fun!—and knew that he'd no right to cause a scene. He stalked away.

"So, Lea, how about that dance?" Quint was smiling, obviously congratulating himself as the winner.

She rounded on him, her expression thunderous. "Where is your date?" Each word was hard as flint.

"Gone to powder her nose. Look, Lea—"

"Find her."

"Lea—"

"No! If you ever want me to speak to you again, not another word!"

Leara didn't wait for Garreth to find her with her drink but went to where he stood by the refreshment table. Wordlessly, he handed her a plastic martini glass filled with bubbling champagne, which she suddenly regretted asking for. He lifted his own glass of Scotch in a toast.

"Here's to the past not repeated," he said quietly, a rueful smile playing around his lips.

Leara nodded and touched her lips to the bubbling amber liquid in her glass. She then lifted her glass and proposed another toast: "And here's to thinking only of this evening . . . and tonight." *And not letting the past spoil the present,* she added silently.

Garreth's eyes darkened, his lids drooping as his gaze moved to her mouth. "Tonight," he agreed and downed his Scotch, neat.

He was caught unaware by a yawn, which he tried to stifle behind his hand. "Think the tennis almost did me in," he admitted.

"How about the football and the sack race and the volleyball? You two were acting like a couple of kids! You're lucky you didn't get a muscle sprain, or throw your back out, or worse!"

He winced. "We were a couple of jerks. I shouldn't have let Lockwood drag me down to his level. But Lea—"

She put her fingers on his lips to still them and shivered lightly as Garreth caught her hand and placed a warm kiss in her palm. "Let's not replay old scenes tonight," he said, unconsciously echoing her earlier thoughts. "Let's write new ones. . . ."

"Hi!" said Chelsea, as she made her way to the refreshment table. "Looks like a good turnout, huh?"

She picked up a chip from an overflowing bowl and eyed the dips.

"Oh, hello, partner," Robert said to Garreth as he joined his wife. He was panting slightly. He and Garreth had been partners in the volleyball contest. "I'm beat—I couldn't last out the song," he said, indicating the fast-tempo Motown hit that was now playing.

"Over the hill," Chelsea said around a mouthful of chip and guacamole. "Next reunion, I'm gonna suggest more sedate stuff. Like horseshoes. Or a rousing game of checkers."

"Not horseshoes," Robert chuckled. "I wouldn't want Garreth or Quint to have something lethal they could throw at each other. My professional services might be needed."

"Leara, how does it feel to be twenty-eight and still have two hunks fighting over you?" Chelsea teased.

"I could live without it," Leara said, embarrassed at the thought that everyone had obviously known what was going on. "How's Amelia?" she asked to steer the conversation away from this afternoon.

Robert and Chelsea groaned simultaneously.

"We placed her in another day care, this week. This was supposed to be someplace special. Robert had to pull all kind of strings just to get her accepted!" Chelsea said. "The second day she was there, I went by a little early to pick her up and found her standing with her nose pressed into the corner—her punishment for jumping up and down instead of standing exactly on her mark as she waited her turn to get a drink of water. Needless to say, I demanded my tuition back and took her home."

"You don't think a child should learn to wait his or her turn?" Garreth was drawn to ask.

"Certainly, but at three and a half a child shouldn't be lined up and expected to be a good little robot,"

Robert replied. "That's too young to master that kind of structure. Leara can tell you."

"Tell me what?" Garreth turned to Leara.

Leara silently blessed Robert for giving her the opening to express her beliefs on child care—and, she hoped, plant some seeds of doubt in Garreth's mind about the care Jenny was receiving from Teagle.

"I can tell you that children master different skills at different ages. I can tell you that nature designed them that way, and if one should try to rush the process, it's usually like putting a tender seedling into hot sunshine—damage is done. Generally, I find no more should be expected of children one and a half to five than for them to learn self-expression and successful social interaction—in other words, how to effectively negotiate for what they want." Leara paused, watching Garreth's face. "In other words, put them together and let them romp and play."

Garreth heard the censure, which had unconsciously crept into Leara's tone. He hadn't a clue as to what was prompting it. "I suppose your baby-sitting experience has taught you a lot about small children," he allowed.

"Baby-sitting . . . ?" Robert and Chelsea chorused, looked at each other, and broke into laughter.

Robert said to Leara, "He doesn't know that you're practically the day care guru of the heartland?"

"Marijo said that you and Leara were just getting back together, Garreth, but you mean you really don't know that Leara's day care centers are regarded as models? I guess you didn't see that article in *Successful Parent* magazine this spring featuring her and her centers?" Chelsea asked.

Garreth turned slowly to Leara, an indefinable expression tightening his features.

She felt oddly embarrassed. "Actually, it's only

three centers, and I have a partner,'' she explained quietly.

Robert said, "But we're trying to talk Leara into expanding to Columbus." Then to Leara, "Have you given it any thought? If you'll consider, we'll personally see that you have all the children you need to fill it, even if we have to go out and canvass the neighborhoods!''

Leara thought of the charming Victorian house she'd seen with Garreth that she'd envisioned as a school. He'd undoubtedly been right—maintenance and utilities alone would be astronomical. Still, the dream had refused to go away. She'd even tentatively broached the idea to her business partner, who had asked pointed questions that had made the idea seem even more impractical.

"I have been thinking of it," she admitted shyly. "But even if my business partner went for the idea, there's a book of regulations two inches thick we'd have to meet. Any location we choose would have to be renovated to comply with them. It would be at least a couple of months before we could get it off the ground.''

Chelsea sighed. "That makes sense. I guess it was just wishful thinking on our parts. But when you do start one, let us know.''

"My daughter Jenny has a nanny. It's more costly, I'm sure, but she gets quality care," Garreth said. "It might be the solution you're looking for.''

"Is Jenny interacting with other children?" Leara immediately queried, biting her tongue in an effort not to say what she thought of the "quality care" Jenny received. No doubt, Garreth would be appalled if he understood the nanny's methods, but she didn't want to make him defensive.

"Social skills can't be learned later. It's a preschool

thing," Robert said. "Most shy adults are said to have had little social interaction with other children as preschoolers. And I know it's important from my personal experience. Before my family moved to Columbus, we had a farm. Nothing around but cornfields. I was an only child, and Mother gave me lots of one-on-one attention, but it was always parent to child. I never learned how to deal with other kids. As a result, I've never felt comfortable with people."

"Robert—you?" Leara asked. "I can't believe that. You've always been the life of the party!"

He grinned, "Yeah. Great defense, huh? I think most comics get their start by feeling socially inept. Instead of going into the entertainment industry, I chose medicine. Doctors being godlike, I don't have to be well adjusted."

As Robert and Chelsea moved on, Garreth sipped his drink, his expression inscrutable.

"What's wrong?" Leara asked at length. Was it what she'd said about child care?

"Who are you?" he asked softly. Where was the girl he remembered?

"I'm the girl you said you loved ten years ago, and the sum of those ten years of living." Leara wondered miserably why she had—unconsciously—encouraged Garreth to fit her into the mold of who he thought she was; of who she used to be.

She shook her head slightly, denying the words that sprang into her mind: *Because somewhere deep in your heart, you never stopped loving him, and you want so very much for it to work this time around. . . .*

Garreth said nothing. Instead, he took her glass from her and put it aside, then folded her into his arms and danced a good part of the evening away.

"Do you see Laurie Ashworth? Over by the statue

and pool?'' Marijo asked sometime later, catching Leara by the hand and turning her.

"No mustache," Leara said sadly, eyeing the woman who'd edged her out for prom queen. "And more gorgeous than high school."

"Do you see that other gorgeous woman, the one she's talking to?" M.J. asked and Leara nodded. "That's her date," M.J. said and flitted off.

Beyond Laurie, Leara saw Quint arguing with a petite brunette. He broke off the argument and started toward Leara. With a feeling of inevitability, she turned to Garreth. "I did promise Quint a dance, and I think he's coming to claim it now."

Garreth stiffened. "If he—"

"No. Don't say anything." She added, "I need to set a few things straight, and this might be a good time. Okay?"

Garreth's fists clenched at his side as Quint pulled Leara onto the dance floor, not bothering to ask her if she wanted to dance.

Quint pulled Leara close, so that she felt the length of him as he moved her gracefully over the floor. She fell into step with him with a naturalness that stunned her. But, on reflection, she realized that they had always danced well together. Quint loved anything that made him the center of attention, and his natural grace made it easy to partner him. He added a couple of fancy ballroom dancing flourishes to the steps as the song ended, and she heard a smattering of applause from the couples surrounding the dance floor.

"You feel good in my arms, Leara," he murmured, holding her close after the music had stopped.

Leara disengaged herself from his grasp and stepped away. She was more annoyed than surprised to find that they had ended up on the opposite side of the dance floor from Garreth—by Quint's design, of course.

"I'm surprised at you, Quint. You're being rude to your date, and that's not like you."

"She's just a friend. Lea—"

"From the way she's looking at you, she'd like to be much more," Leara interrupted.

Quint looked surprised at Leara's comment. He turned and looked again at his date. His mouth drew into a straight line as he turned back to Leara.

"It doesn't matter," he said firmly. "I just want to be with you a few minutes. What's the matter?" he asked, catching her arm as she turned away. His blue eyes sparked with challenge when she started to protest. "Afraid Conroe can't handle the competition? Or maybe you still have feelings for me that you don't want to admit?"

"Quint, you and I are divorced. And I realize now that we can't be friends. As long as I try, you'll never admit that we're through. We never can—"

"If Conroe wasn't interfering—"

"We've been divorced for months, and Garreth had nothing to do with our breakup!" Leara said adamantly, only realizing it was a lie as the words left her mouth. She had dated Quint before she'd known Garreth, true, but Garreth had been the one that she'd fallen in love with. She'd carried that love in a secret place in her heart all these years, never realizing it herself. Had she and Quint ever really had a chance?

She had used Quint's love for her to help her escape all those years ago, then had never been able to give him the love he needed in return. And she couldn't even make it up to him. Encouraging him now wouldn't set him free to find his happiness with someone else.

"Quint, I've told you before—"

Whatever she would have told him was cut off abruptly by a voice on a loudspeaker: "And now, class of eighty-two, we challenge you to a dance contest!"

The voice of Loretta Johnson, former class president, rang out over the room.

"Three songs will be played: slow, medium, and fast. Couples will be judged on skill, originality, and stamina. During the last song, the judges will eliminate couples by touching them on the shoulder. Please leave the floor if this happens to you. When three couples are remaining, a final song will be played to allow time for the judges to make their decisions. Then the couples will line up here, and prizes will be awarded." She paused for the murmuring to die. "Don't be shy, people! I want to see everyone out on that floor."

"C'mon. Let's win this thing!" Quint caught Leara and swung her onto the dance floor.

"I don't want—" She closed her mouth, realizing by his smile that protest was useless.

The tempo of the music was slow and sensual, and Quint seemed intent on melding Leara to himself. With spins and dips he kept her just off balance enough that she couldn't escape the pressure of his body and put some distance between them. She wanted to get away from him, but she couldn't do that without causing a scene. She could swear that she could feel Garreth's eyes on her, but when she looked for him, he was nowhere to be seen.

The band segued into a Latin-flavored melody, and Quint took the cue and moved her to arm's length, hips twisting and feet on the move. "You remember how to do this, love," he said. "That's it!"

She followed his expert lead, reacquainting herself with the steps of the merengue as she continued to look for Garreth. When the dance floor had been cleared of all but a few couples, she located him, her brows riding up in surprise. He was expertly partnering Quint's abandoned date to the hot Latin music.

When Quint felt a tap on the shoulder, he stopped

dancing and turned, expecting to see a judge disqualifying them. He scowled to find Garreth, realizing that Garreth had cost him the contest.

"I believe the ladies want to change partners," Garreth said smoothly, flicking a smile at Fran Carlton before he firmly led Leara away.

"You just cost me five, Conroe. I bet you two would come to blows," a thin man said. Leara couldn't make out the name on his tag. "Just like the prom."

"I'm determined not to repeat the mistakes of the past," Garreth answered, but his words were really for Leara.

"Scotch again?" the man pouring drinks asked. They'd unconsciously stopped near the bar.

"No," Leara laughed, "he's had enough." Her voice dropped, becoming seductively husky. "I don't want you inebriated tonight."

"Why not?" Garreth asked, his eyes glinting darkly as his gaze lingered on her lips. Following his urge, he bent to taste them briefly, thoroughly, and silently damned Lockwood for ever coming between them. "I'm not driving, remember?" He then tilted his head the other way and tasted her lips again.

Leara's laughter tinkled. "I wouldn't want you getting lost on the elevator, either," she said as they moved onto the dance floor.

Quint accepted the drinks from the bartender and turned to hand one to his date, his eyes never leaving the woman in the peach silk dress. She was laughing up at Conroe, leaning close to the jerk. It set his teeth on edge to see them like that. He started to move toward the lobby.

Fran Carlton caught Quint's arm. "Where are you going? I thought we were going to sit down?"

Quint flashed her his best car-salesman smile, but his gaze strayed back to the couple a few feet away that he'd just overheard. "In just a moment. I have to use the phone. Have your drink, okay?"

Finding a house phone, Quint dialed the operator. After a few rings, a harried voice came onto the line.

"Yes. I'd like Garreth Conroe's room."

"I don't have a Garreth Conroe listed."

"I . . . I believe he's staying with Leara Lockwood, or Leara James. Not certain which name the room's under."

"Mr. Conroe is listed as sharing Ms. Lockwood's room. I'll ring the room now, sir."

As he heard the first ring, Quint hung up the phone.

"Did you get through? You look upset," Fran told Quint as he joined her.

"I'll get them later. C'mon, baby. You look tired. I'll take you home."

_____ EIGHT _____

Garreth waltzed Leara out of the elevator and down the corridor, humming a Strauss tune. He loved the way she sparkled when she laughed up at him, her body swaying with his in time to the music. He danced her to the door of her room and bowed to her with a flourish.

"Cinderella, it's nearly midnight." Garreth chuckled low in his throat as he backed Leara up against the door, one hand on her waist, the other cupping her cheek. His eyes were heavy lidded with desire. "If I don't get you into the room, I'll turn into a pumpkin."

"Prince Charming, it's well past one A.M." She was totally aware of the feel of Garreth's hands on her and the hunger surging through her at his touch. It had been so long. . . . Tonight was a fantasy come true!

Leara caught her breath as his mouth was suddenly trailing down her neck to her bare shoulder, his teeth nipping lightly. When he kissed her, she melted against him. Her body was liquid, hot, and yielding. If he hadn't held her pressed between his hardness and the door, her knees would never have supported her.

Unaware of anything but Garreth, Leara wound her

arms around his neck, pulling his mouth more tightly against hers. She opened herself to him, moaning when his tongue invaded, teasing, tasting.

Then, suddenly, the elevator doors opened. Leara heard voices and footsteps. She pushed at Garreth's arms, trying to free herself. "Garreth." The word was garbled by his lips still insistently seeking hers. "Garreth!"

"What?" He seemed dazed, but he pulled away enough for her to slip out of his arms. "Leara?"

Then he heard the voices and glanced down the corridor at the people coming toward them. He grinned crookedly at her, his eyes teasing.

"Just . . . let me find my key," Leara whispered, digging in her handbag. She pulled the keycard out at last and, with a trembling hand, inserted it in the slot. When the little light on the lock flashed green, Garreth reached around her to open the door and ushered her inside.

The room was dark. Leara felt her way to the bedside lamp and switched it on. She turned around to find Garreth right in front of her. She gasped in surprise, the startled rush adding to the beat of her pounding heart.

He put his arms around her and pulled her against him again, smoothing his hands up her back. His fingers found the zipper pull, and he guided it down the track, sliding his other hand under the silk and against her skin.

The feeling was the most sensual he had ever experienced: the cool silk against the back of his hand, the warm satin of her skin against his palm. He tasted her throat again, tilting her head back as he tickled the sweet-salty length with his tongue, then nibbled at the ridge of her jaw. The scent of her heated skin came to him again, all sweetness and musk, and he groaned deep in his throat at the resurgence of desire through his body.

This was a dream come true. Nights of aching for her, years of arms feeling empty, even when someone else filled them. This was Leara. His Leara. The magical princess who had made his youth a joy; whose absence had emptied it of meaning.

"Leara," he murmured fervently against her ear, lifted her into his arms, laid her on the bed.

Leara sat up. "Wait!"

"No." Garreth sat on the bed, pushing her shoulders back against the pillow.

"Garreth."

He paid no attention but began kissing her chest, his lips making little forays down to the top of her dress, where her breasts were aching for his touch.

She drew in a deep, trembling breath and pushed against his shoulders until he reluctantly sat up.

"Garreth. I—uh—I planned for this to be—uh—special." His dark brows rose speculatively and her face turned a soft pink as she went on, "I wanted this to be, well, . . . perfect."

Garreth looked around, suddenly taking in the champagne, the candles. He looked into her face, watched her blush deepen as she tore her eyes from his. She had wanted this all along, had planned the details of a romantic night—and here he'd thought he was going to seduce her! "Honey, you are special," he breathed.

Garreth got up from the bed and crossed the room to the dresser. He pulled the champagne from the bucket, draped a nearby towel over his arm, and bowed slightly. "Care for some wine, my lady?"

The courtly manners he affected made her giggle. She rose from the bed, crossed to the TV, and fiddled with the box on the top until she found a soft rock radio station. There was a sharp pop as Garreth pushed the cork from the champagne bottle. He handed her a filled glass seconds later, his gaze warming her with its promise. Taking his own glass, he moved until they were almost touching, until she could feel the heat of him through her clothes.

Garreth took in every aspect of her. Her tousled curls caressed her soft cheeks, and her silver eyes burned feverishly in the soft light. The shoulders of her dress fell low on her arms, the zipper still loosened. Her breasts rose with every breath, and the tiny points that pressed against the silk invited him to smooth the straps from her creamy shoulders, exposing them to his eyes.

His breath was ragged as he lifted the champagne glass to his lips, the dry taste burning its way down his tight throat.

"More?" His voice caressed her. The question meant more than just an invitation to another glass of champagne. It promised a myriad of new sensations, new experiences. Yes, she wanted more. Much more.

Leara put her glass on the dresser and put her arms around his neck. "I have something to take care of," she murmured to him. "A surprise." Unable to control himself, he pulled her roughly against his body and covered her mouth with his own. She answered him in kind, straining against him, the exquisite sparring making his breath come thick and his heart pound in his ears.

Leara was swept with a dizziness that had nothing to do with the wine. "Garreth," she said, pulling away. "I'll be right back. I have to . . . uh, go."

He was so lost in the sensuous exploration of her shoulders, tasting and nibbling his way from the curve of her neck to the point, it took a moment for her words to register. He reluctantly loosened his hold and stepped back. "If you make me wait too long, I'll come in after you," he growled.

She reached up and planted a light kiss on his lips. "You won't have to wait long. I promise." And she disappeared into the bathroom.

He poured himself another glass of champagne and swallowed half of it. Looking around, he spotted the candles. Sitting on the edge of the turned-down bed, he reached for the box of matches on the bedside table. It fell to the floor, and he eyed it darkly, deciding that he didn't want to expend the energy to pick it up.

"Dark is nice," he mumbled, getting comfortable on the bed. "Real nice," he said, viewing the insides of his eyelids as he decided to rest his eyes for just a moment.

Leara slid the frilly dress to the floor and stepped out of it. The cool air brushed her fevered skin and gooseflesh raised on her skin as her nipples tightened. She pushed the pale pantyhose down her legs. She smiled at her reflection in the mirror. This body definitely belonged to a woman. If Garreth was expecting to see the girl of long ago, well . . . he had a surprise coming.

She hung the dress on the hanger that had held her nightgown. The dress had been a hit. And a bit too much provocation, she chided herself. Quint had found the dress as enticing as Garreth had.

"Garreth, I want to get something out of the way," she called toward the door. "I think you need to know that there's nothing between Quint and me. Nothing at all. I know he can be annoying, but I . . . well, I feel guilty about what I did to him. But he's in the past."

There was no answer from the bedroom. Leara shrugged. Well, she'd tried. If Garreth was still jealous, tonight would surely change his mind.

She dabbed more perfume along her neck and down between her breasts and slid the silver silk nightgown over her head. The fabric clung to her like a second skin, the hard points of her nipples and the indentation of her navel almost more pronounced than if she had been naked.

Looking at her image in the mirror, she felt infinitely desirable, and a tiny bit shy. She slowly opened the bathroom door. The bedroom was dark. The light filtering through the drapes barely illuminated the figure on the bed.

She'd forgotten to light the candles.

She smoothed the gown down her sides, self-consciously, as she stepped into the doorway. The silver silk hissed under her hands.

She slowly moved toward the bed, her body swaying with the sensual feel of the silk sliding against her bare skin and the anticipation of the heat of Garreth's hands touching her through the slick fabric.

Why didn't he say something? His face was in shadow, but she could swear that she felt his eyes devouring her. She moved around the bed and stood next to him. When he didn't move, she sat on the edge of the bed. Her hip was pressed against his thigh.

But no large hands reached out for her, pulling her against him. No warm lips found her skin.

"Garreth?" she whispered. Leara touched his face lightly, running the tips of her fingers over his features.

His eyes were closed.

Leara reached over and snapped on the light. Garreth lay completely relaxed against the pillows. His chest's slowly rising and falling was the only indication that he still lived. A champagne glass had fallen onto the sheet, spilling a few drops of wine.

Leara didn't know whether to be angry or hurt or to laugh out loud. She touched one of his dark curls, and Garreth stirred, grumbled, and pulled a pillow around under his head, still totally asleep.

She snapped the light off. Going around to the other side of the bed, she crawled in and pulled the covers over them both, snuggling against his broad back. She snaked her hand around his waist, tucking her fingers into the opening in his shirt, caressing him lightly.

"Well, I just hope you don't snore," Leara murmured to his unconscious form.

NINE

Garreth cracked open one eye, and the muted light coming through a crack in the drapes painfully stabbed it. His lid dropped as if weighted.

It was warm in the bed. Pleasant. If he could just ignore the cotton in his mouth, he might get back to sleep. The pillow was soft under his head, the covers were soft against his arm. And that warm arm around his—

Arm?

The memory was slow in returning. Leara? Yes. It had to be. He had a vague memory of waltzing her to the room.

He cracked open the eye again and forced himself to look at the room. Candles. A champagne flute. Yes! Now he remembered. The champagne. On top of Scotch. He and Leara had come up to her room. . . .

He was in bed with Leara!

What had happened? He searched his memory. There was nothing but a blank after Leara had gone into the bathroom to change. Was it possible that they had made love and he didn't remember?

117

The arm across him moved. Garreth turned slowly onto his back, savoring the feel of Leara's silky hand sliding along his belly. And his body flared to life.

Turning his head, Garreth gazed down on the beautiful woman slumbering beside him. Her copper curls flamed against the white of the pillowcase. Her long-lashed eyes were tightly closed, their silver depths hidden. Cheeks pink with sleep; full, moist lips open slightly; fingers of one hand curled beside her head; she looked more wonderful than even in his most vivid dreams.

A painful tenderness gripped him. This was what he wanted more than anything. He wanted to wake up beside this woman every day for the rest of his life. Garreth leaned toward her. He could feel her breath on his face, see her eyes fluttering to life, hear the soft sigh that soughed from her mouth just as his own descended to claim it.

Leara sighed under his lips. His warm mouth had closed over hers just as she had become aware of him beside her. Now, her body sprang into an awareness so pleasurable that she moaned. She opened her mouth to surrender to his probing tongue and to meet it with her own.

Her next awareness was of his hands caressing her, his body pressed so tightly to her that she could barely take a breath. Heat seemed to surge between them, building until the restricting covers had to be thrown off.

Garreth forgot about the slight headache he'd awakened with. Instead, he was exhilarated, his body filled with power. Raised on one elbow, he looked down at Leara.

Her eyes were dark with emotion, keeping their secrets from him. But her body told him everything. Her hands were restless, stroking his chest as she exposed it by unbuttoning his shirt. Her breasts rose and fell rapidly as panting breaths grazed the hand he caressed her face with.

The silver silk gown that she wore was pulled low across her breasts, the tiny straps straining into her shoulders. Barely covered by the silk, her erect nipples were outlined by the fabric, teasing him, tempting him to cover them with his hands, his mouth.

Leara was suddenly drowning in sensations. The taste of Garreth on her lips, the feel of his hot fingers sliding over her aching silk-clad skin, the pungency of his male scent, the crisp coarseness of the hair under her fingers as she snaked her hand over his chest. She was drowning, too, in the promise his eyes held. They were dark with desire, but there was more there; the tenderness she saw in his face couldn't be hidden by the twisting passion. The boy she had loved, who had loved her, still felt for her as he had.

The phone ringing insistently brought Leara out of the trance in which Garreth's eyes had held her. She started to reach over him to answer it. Garreth was unwilling to let her. He was immersed in Leara, her beauty, her softness, her touch. He rolled her onto her back, covering her with his body. He rocked his arousal against her, pouring out words into her ears. "Leara. Leara. Love, I want you so much. God! Nothing else could ever be as right as this!"

The phone continued its insistent jangle. "Garreth. Garreth! The phone."

Garreth's lips were against the softness of her breast, his tongue lapping at her tangy skin. "Let it ring," he mumbled. "It'll stop."

Her own body pleaded with her to ignore everything except the sensations that were coursing through her. But, as the phone rang again, she remembered that only one or two people knew where to reach her, and if one of them was calling her here, it had to be something that couldn't wait.

She rolled over and picked up the receiver.

"Hello?"

"Leara? Were you in the shower or something? You took so long to answer the phone, I almost gave up." It was her business partner, Becky Taylor, and she sounded upset.

Garreth hadn't stopped his exploration of Leara's softness when she answered the phone. She now caught his hands, frowning, and he reluctantly ceased.

"Becky? It's—" She checked the travel clock on the bedside table. "Only five thirty. What could you possibly want this early? And on a Sunday." She felt as though her friend must be able to hear her pounding heart over the phone.

"Five thirty? I didn't realize—" Her voice was strained with weariness. "I've been up half the night. The Kramer Street center caught fire last night. Luckily someone in the neighborhood was still up and saw the fire right after it began, about 2:45 this morning. The sprinkler system probably saved the structure, but the damage looks so bad!" Becky let out a huge sigh that was the epitome of disappointment. "Leara, the fire marshals have been at it ever since the fire was put out. They're saying it was arson."

"Arson?" Leara sat on the edge of the bed. As Garreth listened to Leara's end of the conversation, a frown grew between his brows.

Leara listened a few moments more as Becky told her of the damage from the fire and the huge mess left in the wake of the firemen and their hoses, then she broke in: "Have you thought about Monday morning? We need to make plans—we've got nearly a hundred kids due to come in! The first thing is to start calling parents and staff—thank God our enrollment records are in the computer at the Brook Street center. Look, I'm leaving right away. You go back home—you sound exhausted. There's nothing you can do there, at least for now. I'll be there as soon as I can.'' She shivered involuntarily and Garreth rubbed her upper arms to warm her. ''You try to catch a couple of hours' sleep. We'll solve this together.'' Her voice held more confidence than she felt.

After Leara hung up the phone, she started bustling around the room, gathering her things, throwing clothes in her suitcase as she answered Garreth's puzzled questions, explaining what had happened.

''I can help. I know a reliable contractor in Gary, but the first thing is getting the debris cleared away—''

''Garreth!'' Leara interrupted. Her mind was whirling. There was so much to do! ''Garreth, thank you, but no. I . . . I don't know just what I need to do first. Other than get to Gary and assess the situation.''

''Then I'll go with you and help,'' he said firmly, getting out of bed.

''No!''

The strength of her objection startled her as much as Garreth. Looking anywhere but in his eyes, she stammered, ''It's wonderful of you to offer. Really. But you . . . would be . . . a . . . distraction.'' As her eyes pleaded with him to understand, she added silently, *I can't think straight when you are around. All I can do is feel. Wonderful feelings, overwhelming feelings. And right now, I need a clear head—and don't look at me as if I'm a child asking to cross the street for the first time!*

She turned to put more clothes into the suitcase. ''I hope you don't mind,'' she said as silence between them lengthened.

I do mind! he thought in exasperation, watching her efficient movements. He wondered where the sexy, warm, kittenish Leara had vanished to so quickly. Even though her tousled hair and flushed face still reminded him of watching her wake next to him, even though her body was still barely concealed by the slinky silk gown, she might as well have been wearing a bun and a power suit!

This was the stranger he'd glimpsed last evening. Where was the woman he knew? It confounded him. He ran a hand through his hair and noticed the slight headache he'd awakened with was returning.

"Leara, I . . . I'll be here when you need me. As soon as you finish taking stock of the damage, call."

"I'll call if I need you—damn, where is my other earring?"

Disgruntled, Garreth watched Leara dive back into the bathroom in search of her lost earring, feeling— accurately—that he'd already been dismissed from her thoughts.

Leara sagged into the wingback chair, running a hand through her hair. She rested her head against the high back, closed her eyes, and a deep sigh escaped her. *I could sleep right here,* she thought.

The phone rang, shattering the quiet in her small apartment. Leara groaned. She opened one eyelid, just a fraction, and eyed the instrument with disdain as she awaited her answering machine to pick up the call. As a deep voice began to leave a message after the beep, she picked up the receiver, a slight frown gathering between her brows.

"Garreth, I'm here. Hello."

"Leara? I'm glad I finally caught you at home. I've called every night this week. How are you?"

"Tired."

"You sound it."

Leara closed her eyes and savored the warm caring

in his voice. "Look, I've gotten your messages, but I've been getting in so late. . . ." The excuse sounded lame to her own ears. She didn't know why she'd been avoiding returning his calls. She hadn't spoken to Garreth since she'd returned to Gary. Well, she'd been busy. . . .

"You must be running yourself ragged."

"This last week has been a marathon. Luckily, the damage from the fire isn't as bad as we first thought."

At Leara and Becky's first inspection, they had been stunned by the great black hole in the ceiling, kitchen equipment melted and twisted by heat, and the black ooze—smoke and ash mixed with water—which was everywhere, dripping from the ceiling, covering the floor, everywhere. The designs on the soles of the firemen's rubber boots were imprinted in the muck on the floor in what looked like a formal pattern.

Leara had been surprised when closer examination by the insurance adjuster and the city building inspector had shown the integrity of the structure was fine. Leara continued, "There have been a million details to take care of and a million insurance forms to fill out—I swear, I filled out one yesterday that confirmed that I had filled out a form to confirm that we had filed a claim!"

Garreth's deep chuckle soothed her frayed nerves and filled her with a sense of well-being. Why had she been avoiding talking to him, anyway?

"You should have called me. I could have had my secretary in Chicago take care of those. Have the insurance people given you the go-ahead to start cleanup and repairs? I called Bill Hoffpaur this morning. He's working a big job on the other side of Gary right now, but he could spare a few men with his best foreman to start your project . . . Leara? Are you still there?"

Leara sighed deeply. "I was just remembering something I'd forgotten." Like why she hadn't called him.

"He can have a crew at your loca—"

"Garreth, I've already hired a contractor. The work is under way."

There was a period of silence. Leara looked at the receiver and bit her lip, holding back the urge to tell him that this contractor was someone they'd used before, one that was familiar with the state regs concerning day care centers—to rush words into the silence to soothe any miffed feelings she'd caused.

"I don't understand, Leara. All I'm doing is offering my expertise."

Her control snapped.

"It would be nice if you'd realize that I'm a big girl now. I can cross the street all by myself. I can fill out those confusing old insurance forms, and if I have trouble, I can even call my insurance agent and have her clarify a point. I can run a business, make decisions, even—*Oh, damn!*" She drew in a ragged breath and exhaled in an exasperated gust.

"Look. I'm sorry. Don't—I'm just tired. Okay?"

"Leara, I felt I had something to offer. I never meant to offend—"

"Garreth, I have been recognized for my expertise in a certain area. Child care. Have you taken my advice?"

"What are you talking about?"

"Where is Jenny right now?"

"Asleep. Wh—"

"Who tucked her into bed?"

"Mrs. Teagle. She was already in bed when I got home. What are you—"

"Mrs. Teagle reads to Jenny every night when she tucks her into bed. She reads exactly three pages. Never more or less. Mrs. Teagle takes Jenny to the park and kindly allows her to sit on the bench and watch while she knits. Jenny is afraid to get down from the bench and play—and it's not shyness. Mrs. Teagle dresses Jenny every morning in pretty clothes that her father will like, and if she should get a spot of chocolate milk or drip of ice cream or a smudge of dirt on her pretty clothes, Mrs. Teagle kindly lets Jenny know that her daddy might not love her if she's less than a perfect little lady.

"Garreth, I used a great deal of constraint the other night at the dance, but I wasn't talking about child care in general so much as I was trying to get it across to you that all is not well in regard to the care your daughter is receiving. This fire has given me a lot of headaches right now—not the smallest of which is the fact that it was arson." *And seems to have been aimed at me personally,* Leara thought to herself and shivered slightly as she remembered the garbled, hate-filled message that had been on her answering machine when she got back from Columbus. "But the main thing keeping me awake at night is thinking of Jenny at the mercy of that harpy. I blame myself," she went on. "I should have just told you: lose the Teagle. And don't tell me how she's cared for the children of some of the aristocratic families in Europe; when they figured out her method of emotional blackmail to maintain control, they probably had her deported! So, lose the Teagle. Teagle could never pass the psychological evaluation we give all our employees. Lose the Teagle before she does damage that can never be undone!"

After several moments of silence, Garreth spoke, his voice very soft. "How can what you say be true? Jenny is very attached to her nanny."

Leara closed her eyes. From the slightly questioning tone in his voice, she knew that she had gotten through. "Spend more time with Jenny. Take over some of her care, yourself. Get another live-in sitter—but beware of too much perfection. Children are messy, curious, inconvenient, wonderful little creatures. I have a feeling Mrs. Teagle's main efforts at job security have been to make your household run like clockwork. Most important—'' the lamp she was staring at blurred as tears welled up in Leara's eyes, ''get to know who . . . who your daughter is.'' As her own father had never put out the effort or taken the time to get to know her.

''That's my assessment, Garreth. I know you didn't ask for it, but I'm offering my expertise.''

Leara placed the phone back in its cradle, not waiting for his reply. She'd call him back tomorrow.

''Tomorrow is another day, Scarlett, so let's get some sleep,'' she said wearily and rose and turned off the lamp.

Leara was awakened the next morning by someone impatiently pounding on her door.

''I don't believe this!'' she muttered, rolling over and pulling the pillow over her head. Peeking from under it at her bedside clock, she saw it was eight A.M. and groaned.

''No! I'm not here! Go away!'' She pulled the pillow tighter. She'd turned off her alarm before going to bed, turned off the ringers on her phones, and had made firm plans to sleep until noon. ''Have some mercy. It's Saturday, for Chrissakes!''

The knocking continued at intermittent intervals. Someone was letting her know that he wasn't going away.

Leara bore the annoyance as long as possible before she reluctantly gave up her warm cocoon, throwing the covers off and crawling out of bed. Keeping the chain on, she opened her door and peered out. Sherry brown eyes met hers. She closed her eyes and counted to five aloud. Opening them again, she said, "You're really here."

Garreth held up a white box. "I brought doughnuts for breakfast. May I come in?"

"If I closed the door again, would you continue to stand out here and knock?"

"Yes. Since I've brought food, I could last all day."

"You wouldn't consider passing those doughnuts through the crack without me taking the chain off?"

"No. And know what? These are chocolate with vanilla custard filling. The filling is still warm. I waited while they were being iced."

Leara unhooked the chain and swung the door wide. "Come in, rat. Make yourself at home—and hand over those doughnuts."

As Garreth stepped inside, Leara relieved him of the doughnuts, fished one out of the box, and sank her teeth into it. "Mmmmm. This is so good, it should be illegal," she said and drifted into the kitchenette to make coffee.

Garreth looked around the surprisingly sterile apartment. Everything was scrupulously neat. Two leather wingback chairs flanked a sofa of the same color. The coffee table held a pair of picture books. The TV was an older model. The picture behind the sofa was a lithograph of Monet's *Waterlilies*. Nowhere were there photos or mementos, no clutter of personal items. The apartment had about as much personality as a doctor's waiting room. The only thing of Leara in the apartment was her grandmother's hutch, which was wedged into a corner.

"Coffee will be a sec," Leara said, returning. She bit into another creme-filled doughnut, closed her eyes in contentment, and licked the creme from her lips.

Watching her innocently provocative gesture, Garreth felt heat rush to his loins. She looked like a nymph.

Her coppery curls were thoroughly tousled, framing her face. Her cheeks were rosy, her gray eyes dark and languorous. Several of the tiny buttons closing the front of her wholly feminine cotton print and eyelet night-gown were undone, and the gown had slipped to the side, exposing one satin shoulder that he longed to kiss.

"Where is your suitcase?" he asked gruffly.

Leara blinked. "Why?"

"You can pack while the coffee's brewing."

"Pack?"

"I'm taking you to Chicago for the weekend," Garreth said as he strode down the short hallway to her bedroom.

"But I haven't agreed to go to Chicago with you! I have things to do—"

"Nothing that can't wait. Remember, it's the Fourth of July weekend. I'm going to a Cubbies game and I'm taking you with me. And I have specific orders from Kimmi to bring her back a game ball."

"So you got my address from Marijo."

"And she's keeping Jenny." Garreth firmly forbade his thoughts to stray to the bed, to Leara in that bed, but not before he noticed how the sheets were rumpled. They were probably still warm. . . .

"I can't just leave! I have a million things to do."

"You can't do much before Monday. Now, where's a suitcase?"

Leara opened a closet and pulled one out. "Here," she glared. "You pack it. If I'm going to be kidnapped, I need a cup of coffee."

Garreth chuckled as Leara, muttering, went back to the kitchen. He pulled open a drawer and a froth of lacy underthings foamed out, and he drew in a deep breath.

TEN

"What a gorgeous view." Leara turned her face into a gust of wind off the lake, breathing deeply of the cool, moist air and crossing her arms against its slight chill. Below them, traffic was heavy along Michigan Avenue. Cars edged the lake with a moving, almost unbroken ring of lights. The dark face of the water was sprinkled with a scattering of navigation lights and the running lights of a few boats coming in late to harbor. "What are you doing in there, anyway?"

"Nothing." Garreth smiled secretly as he came up behind her and wrapped his arms around her, sliding his hands along her chilled upper arms and smoothing away the goose bumps he found there.

"Mmmm. That's nice." She tilted her head back, resting it against his shoulder. "I hadn't remembered the wind off the lake felt so cool."

"Do you want a sweater?"

"I don't think you packed one for me," Leara said dryly.

Garreth chuckled, remembering her consternation when she'd opened her suitcase and a froth of lingerie had boiled out. "I packed things I wanted to see you in—hold still," he said as he tried to nuzzle her ear. "Your ear has some chill bumps on it, poor little thing. I have to kiss it and make it warm." His lips found her earlobe, but a coppery curl persisted in tickling his nose. He gave up on the ear and kissed the curl.

Closing his eyes, he pulled her more firmly against his chest, savoring the feel of her in his arms. Was it only weeks ago that his life had seemed so unbalanced? For a long time, he'd felt a vague dissatisfaction, but he'd had no idea what it was all about. He'd achieved success, he was living the American dream—all his carefully laid career plans had come to fruition. And it hadn't been enough. Until he'd found Leara again.

Shy, gentle, kind, beautiful. He'd never stopped loving this woman. He'd never stopped damning himself for letting her go. And he'd never willingly let her go again.

"Well, considering I now have the choice of three silk teddies, two garter belts, and four nightgowns, and no spare bras, I'd say I'll be spending a great deal of time in our room," she groused good-naturedly. "It's sheer luck that I picked up my garment bag." She'd never gotten around to unpacking it after the reunion trip last weekend and it still contained her favorite slacks outfit and the peach silk dress she'd worn to the reunion. "I don't think hotel café staff would appreciate my coming down to breakfast in that fire-engine-red negligee."

"I started to just pack your toothbrush. But I found that gown hidden in the bottom of the drawer. I've been thinking about it all afternoon—I thought the Cubs game would never end. All through the extra innings, I was imagining taking that red silk off you," he murmured near her ear and was rewarded when she shivered lightly.

"I'm glad you kidnapped me. This is nice."

Garreth smiled into wind-whipped curls. "I'm glad you approve. I must confess to ulterior motives."

"Mmmm. The best kind." She turned in his arms. "What were they?"

"You mean are they.'" He waggled his brows in an exaggerated leer and she giggled.

"Has it got something to do with what you were doing inside the room?"

"I'm not telling." Garreth stroked her hair softly. "You must have had one hell of a week. When I spoke with you on the phone last night, you sounded ready to drop—even before you got mad at me. So, I've tried to provide what you appeared to need most—a carefree afternoon." He congratulated himself, because it appeared to have worked. Leara had come to life, her cheeks flushed with excitement as she'd cheered her Cubbies or booed a call she disagreed with. Now, as she turned in his arms to face him, she was relaxed, smiling.

"I want to hear more about the ulterior part." Leara placed her hands softly on each side of his face. His cheeks were scratchy with the day's growth of beard. She scraped her palms against the lightly bristled skin, reveling in the sensuous feel.

Her hands moved to undo the buttons of his shirt. Surprised and pleased by her boldness, Garreth stood immobile under her spell as she pulled it free from the waistband of his jeans, and her fingers explored his firm pecs, the muscles covering his ribs, his taut stomach.

"My ulterior motive is quite simple. I'm going to take you to bed and let you have your way with me."

She raised her face, her eyes glowing. "Exactly what do you think I'm— Look!" She pointed suddenly as the first rocket of the Fourth of July fireworks display exploded in a golden ball over the lake; then that ball exploded into more spheres of red, white, and blue.

"Beautiful," he whispered, ignoring the fiery barrage exploding in the night sky. His eyes were only for Leara. "We can stay here, or we can watch the fireworks from inside." His voice was gruff with desire.

The look in his eyes was almost black, sparkling with the reflected star bursts exploding over the water. Looking into them sent flames of desire running through her, sparkling along her nerve endings like the golden bursts overhead. "I think seeing the fireworks from inside will be much more interesting," she breathed.

Garreth bent and kissed her deeply. Without taking his lips from hers, he hooked an arm beneath her knees, lifted her, and carried her inside. As he lowered her to her feet, she savored the feel of her body sliding along his hard, muscled frame.

His mouth claimed hers in another brief, hard kiss. "God, how I've wanted this," he said softly. He looked down in wonder as his hands moved up and down her torso. "The feel of you is so familiar, it's like reliving a sweet dream. But this is no dream. You're here in my arms."

She leaned back, eyes closed. The top button of her blouse had come undone and the shadowy cleft between her breasts seemed to beckon to him. He leaned her further, still, supporting her with an arm beneath her shoulders. He was distantly aware of her choked sigh as his lips and tongue tasted the tender skin revealed in the vee of her blouse.

Garreth lifted his head and raised her hand to further undo the buttons of her blouse, but he found her hands already at the buttons. She slipped the fabric from her shoulders and it whispered as it fell to the floor. Her bra followed and was soon joined by her jeans. His gaze was as tangible as a caress, as it moved over every part of her. Maturity had made her bottom slightly more rounded and her breasts slightly fuller. Her nipples seemed to throb visibly as he touched them, and the sound of Leara's gasp of pleasure sent a surging pleasure washing through him. His mouth closed over first one tight pink bud and then the other, and she arched into the contact, clinging to his wide shoulders for support.

Garreth lay her gently on the bed and reached for a box of matches. It was then she noticed the candles on the bedside tables. "I picked them up after you left our hotel room in Columbus. They seemed to symbolize something unfinished."

"Then come to bed."

She watched as he slipped out of his shirt, then loosened his belt and unfastened his jeans. But she was unwilling to remain a passive observer. Sitting upright, she reached out and helped pull the jeans down.

His hands settled restlessly at his sides, inviting her to complete what she had started. With shaking hands, she stroked his chest and stomach, skimmed over his hips, and slipped her hands inside the waistband of his briefs and removed them also.

She stroked the insides of his lightly furred thighs, enjoying the feel as his muscles bunched and hardened under her fingers. As her fingers closed over his jutting, velvet-covered shaft, she heard his sharp intake of breath and looked up as she began to slowly, sensuously stroke it. Star bursts from the fireworks filled the sky behind Garreth. The flickering candles revealed his rigid, passion-filled features, his eyes black beneath heavy, half-closed lids. The look in them was utterly compelling.

In the space of a breath, he was beside her. Her body pressed into him as he kissed her fingertips, one by one, then nipped at the fleshy mound at the base of her thumb.

"Garreth! Now! I feel like I'm coming apart."

With difficulty, Garreth held himself in check. Leara's softness was pressed to him, and when her belly brushed against his erection, his whole body throbbed.

Leara moaned as Garreth's mouth covered hers hungrily. As he probed her open mouth with his tongue, she pulled his head closer. The fires his hands created everywhere they touched drove her to press her body even more tightly to his. Her nipples contracted with tingling pleasure created by the rough caress of his chest hair. When Garreth slid his hands over her buttocks and lifted her hips against his hardness, she broke the kiss and whimpered against his neck as she was almost carried away on the golden swirl surging through her.

"Please."

He pulled away for a moment, picking up a foil packet on the nightstand. Leara caught his hand. "Let me," she said softly.

He groaned as she smoothed the protective sheath over him, then stroked him. He caught her shoulders before he exploded. He realized his Cinderella had grown up.

Garreth lay back and, catching Leara's waist, lifted her astride his hips. And her world erupted into a blaze of sensation.

As her hips began to move in that eternal, internal rhythm, he lifted his hips to meet her, making each thrust deeper, more complete. In seconds, her gasps became moans and she cried his name again and again as they moved together, blazing hotter and brighter as they shot skyward, ever joining and retreating. Dazzling light flashed all around as they exploded together in a magical star burst, shattering into a million brilliant fragments high above the earth.

Clinging tightly together as the shimmering died, they fell through the night sky and softly landed. For long minutes, Garreth held Leara close to him, his heart still soaring. For the first time in years, he felt complete.

"What are you thinking?" she whispered.

"Just like a woman," he chuckled.

"Well?"

His kissed her damp temple. "I'm thinking you're not my Cinderella anymore, but the slipper still fits."

A gentle breeze blew in through the still-open balcony doors, teasing a lock of hair that curled tightly against Leara's cheek. Propped above her on an elbow, Garreth gently smoothed the curl behind her ear—an incredibly sexy ear, he decided. And he smiled as he watched her sleep. Her face was turned slightly away from him, her hand lay curled on the pillow beside her cheek, her fingers closed. The hair about her face, dampened by perspiration during their lovemaking, had formed into tight curls. She looked soft and womanly and vulnerable in the half light.

Loving her had been incredible. Leara had surprised and delighted him with her aggressive demands, and remembering, Garreth was surprised to feel himself spring rigidly to life again so soon afterward. He longed to pull her to him and again sink himself into her warmth, even though this wasn't quite the same woman he'd been dreaming of for ten years.

Perhaps "woman" was the key word. Leara had grown up. She'd become self-sufficient, with a sense of self-worth. Not that he hadn't loved the old Leara, but sometimes she had been just a little too malleable, a little too easy to please. Garreth thought of the warm, generous nature of the woman he'd seen playing with his daughter at the reunion. She hadn't really changed, but she had blossomed and grown since she'd escaped her domineering father.

Guilt niggled at him because he hadn't been the one to help when she'd made that break. If he hadn't been so self-absorbed, they could have had years together.

Leara stirred in her sleep, rolling onto her side. Garreth slipped farther down into the bed, careful not to wake her. He kissed the point of her shoulder, then fitted his chest against her back, circling her waist with his arm.

He had loved her ten years ago. He hadn't even realized how much until she'd gone away with Quint. The memory of that pain made Garreth tighten his hold on Leara, as if assuring himself that she was really with him now.

The hurt had been quickly overshadowed by anger—at Leara, then at himself. As he admitted that he had been ultimately to blame, he'd lost all anger at Leara. He'd thought that never seeing her again would be his punishment.

In frustration, Garreth had applied his driving energy to finishing college, then building a reputation as an architect. For years, he hadn't mentioned Leara's name. Garreth realized now that it had all been useless. He had never been able to erase his need for this woman, only to deny it—and that only until he saw her again.

He thought back to his marriage. Leara's presence had always been there between them, though Marlene hadn't seemed to notice. He wondered if he had married Marlene because she had been much too involved in her modeling career and her dreams of being an actress to demand more than a superficial relationship with him.

The marriage had been a mistake. Jenny was the only good thing that he and Marlene had ever produced. When they'd divorced, there had never been any question about who would get custody of Jenny. Marlene was too self-absorbed to give Jenny the care she needed.

Garreth admitted that he hadn't been such a hot parent, either. He got angry with himself for not seeing how his daughter had been manipulated. If Leara hadn't come back, he'd never have suspected that Teagle wasn't good for Jenny—the salvo Leara had hit him with on the phone last night had really taken him by surprise. And he should have seen it sooner, if he hadn't let himself accept the convenience of leaving the main part of his daughter's care to Teagle.

After Leara had opened his eyes, he'd knocked on Teagle's bedroom door and given the woman a month's severance pay, informing her that her services were no longer needed. Next week, he'd start looking for a good day care—but only for a half day. From now on, he was going to be a full-time father.

He thought of his own parents. His ever-correct, socially oriented mother and business-first father were now retired to Florida. How many times, as he was warming up at a football game, had he scanned the stands and known that sinking feeling when he realized that his father wasn't there? And he'd been on his way to being the same type of father to Jenny!

Then his Leara had come back, and everything was right again. . . . *God, how right it was!*

Garreth smiled into Leara's hair. They would make children—if she wanted children. Knowing Leara, she did. It took a great deal of restraint on his part not to kiss her awake and work toward that goal immediately.

Propping on one elbow, he smoothed the same

springy curl away from her cheek again as he studied her profile in the half light. "I love you, Leara James," he told her softly and kissed the warm pulse at her temple.

ELEVEN

"This is good," Leara said and sipped a steaming cup of espresso. "Perfect after that Black Forest torte." She sighed. "Chicken cacciatore, fajitas, sweet and sour pork—Garreth, I can't believe how many calories I've consumed this afternoon! I feel too heavy to get out of this chair."

They had spent a pleasant afternoon exploring Chicago's International Food Festival, wandering between the booths set up at the lake shore and sampling dishes that had caught their interest. Now, sitting across from her at a small table, Garreth was only vaguely aware of the many people milling between the booths and the tempting aromas permeating the warm air. He was enjoying the play of sunlight and wind in Leara's hair and how her eyes twinkled as she smiled.

"And what is that *look* about? Like the Cheshire cat—you're smiling, but you're not really here," Leara said.

His smile deepened, creating creases, like brackets on each side of his mouth. His sherry brown eyes twinkled warmly as he admitted, "I was just wondering how I can get you to move back to Columbus, so that we can be together more often. I've been relatively free this last month; more or less between projects. But an office building I designed will be going up in the Fort Worth area, with construction starting at the end of July. A Japanese firm has hired us to design a new mall for Calgary, Canada. There's another project coming up on the Coast. Although the firm has a small jet, which cuts down time in airports, I'll still be away from home quite a bit. And whenever I'm free, I'll be dividing my time between Jenny in Columbus and you in Gary. Unless I can talk you into moving closer. Like, into my bedroom.''

"You certainly know how to sweep a girl off her feet with sweet talk—*move in with me, so I can save fuel and time. It would be so much more convenient!*''

"I did that badly, huh?'' Garreth said ruefully, catching her hand.

As his thumb stroked the soft skin across her knuckles, Leara remembered their incredible lovemaking as the Fourth of July rockets had burst over the lake. They had made love twice more during the night. After that first swift slaking of their desire, they had loved slowly—each time teasing one another to greater passion. And she smiled a woman's smile. "Some of your persuasive techniques haven't exactly left me cold,'' she murmured.

"Is that a yes?''

Leara shook her head regretfully. "Not in your bedroom.'' *Not yet*, she added silently. Garreth didn't really know who she was now. And she was finding out the man she'd once known so well had changed, too. Become deeper. More sensitive. Success no longer seemed to be the beacon it had once been to him, blinding him to all else—he no longer seemed to be trying to emulate his workaholic father. Perhaps, now, they did have a chance—if they took it slowly. If they didn't make too many demands of each other too soon.

She gnawed her underlip a moment, then confessed, "No. I won't move in with you. Not right now, anyway. But I have been thinking of expanding the day care business to Columbus—from what I've discovered, there is quite a demand." Speaking hurriedly at first, feeling strangely exposed as she revealed her dream, Leara explained her plans to convert the large turn-of-the-century house they'd seen on Bartholomew Street into a day care and multifunctional learning center, which would deal with everything from tutoring grade-school children after school to offering adult education classes at night. As Leara expanded on her plans, she became more animated, eyes glowing with excitement as she envisioned the finished facility.

Garreth listened quietly, aware of the excitement in her but asking few questions. Sensing that for some reason this project she was planning was very important to her, he didn't tell her all the obvious drawbacks he saw with it. He reminded himself firmly that Leara was intelligent enough to see those for herself. It was even possible, he thought ruefully, that she'd resent it if he pointed out that the building would have to be rewired, it would have to be replumbed with child-sized toilets and basins, and drywalls or something else would have to cover up walls bearing eighty or so years of lead-based paint.

"Yes, I know a more modern building would be more practical," she said, reading the expression in his eyes. "But, can you see it, Garreth?" she asked almost shyly. "Won't it be wonderful?"

"Anything that brings you back to Columbus will be more than wonderful," he fibbed, knowing that the truth would only put a damper on her joy. "Leara, I want to be with you every moment I can. If you—"

What he'd been about to say was interrupted by a series of sharp, insistent beeps. Unclipping a beeper from his belt, Garreth shut it off and frowned at the number it displayed. "It's a Chicago number—but not one of my partner's, or even Marlene's." He looked around. People, booths, food. No possibility of a phone.

Realizing the problem, Leara rose. "Let's get back to the room. It may be important."

"I doubt it," Garreth said rising. "But, even if it's not, there are certain other attractive aspects to going back to our room." He placed his arm around her shoulders, pulling her near as they walked.

"There are no messages," Garreth said, rejoining Leara after inquiring at the hotel's main desk. "If Teresa had needed to get in touch with me, she would have left a message. So, whoever beeped me, it can't be that important."

Garreth's beeper had gone off twice more before they could walk the several blocks back to their hotel, as if it was extremely important that someone get in touch with him. When he'd used the house phone in the lobby to call the number in his beeper, there'd been no answer.

As they got on the elevator, Garreth said, "If anything came up that's urgent, my answering service will have contacted Teresa as well as beeped me. And Teresa would have left some message at the desk, so . . ."

The elevator door closed and Garreth was suddenly much more interested in the darkening of Leara's eyes than in what he'd been saying. He debated whether he should kiss her, and possibly shock the elevator's only other passenger, a little old lady in a passion-purple top and pants.

"So, it probably isn't important at all. Except . . ."

"Except?"

The door opened. After a final curious glance, the older lady exited. The door closed, leaving them alone. "Except," Leara smiled, "I was wondering how to maneuver you back to the hotel room so I could have a nap." She smiled archly. "Someone kept waking me up last night."

"My dear," Garreth said as he flattened his palms on the wall on either side of her face, effectively trapping her, "all you had to say was that you'd like to go to bed."

Leara felt a consuming warmth radiating from Garreth. He stood close, aware of the power his nearness had over her. She could feel the tickle of his breath on her neck, and at that slight sensation, every nerve ending sprang to attention. But he made no move to touch her. The tension slowly built inside her, her breasts tingled, seeming to strain to be pressed again to his chest.

"Garreth . . ." Leara spoke his name like an incantation. Her eyes were deep and smoky in the dimness. Her oval face and short, straight nose accented an almost too full, too tempting mouth.

At first, he touched her only with his lips. The touch was high voltage. With a groan, Garreth pressed her against the side of the elevator, their mouths melding. Garreth quested with his tongue. Leara trembled as he thrust it between her parted teeth, probing the ridges and spaces. Her own tongue answered his, pushing and teasing. The knot of warm ache in her belly unraveled and spread its heat through her. The fire overpowered her, making her dizzy. She felt consumed by it, by the urgency rising in her, by the flame of his hands moving over her shoulders and over her breasts.

The bell dinged and Garreth broke away, crossing

his arms over his chest and tapping his foot as he waited for the doors to open, the picture of nonchalance.

"Oh, you, you—" Leara gasped and frantically straightened her blouse and smoothed her hair and tried to match his aplomb. She received curious looks from the people entering the elevator as she and Garreth got off, and when she reached their room, she discovered why—her lipstick was smeared almost to the dimple in her cheek.

"You!" She threw a pillow at a chuckling Garreth. He ducked, then surged across the bed to tackle her around the knees, bringing her down rather soundly atop him.

Leara lay across his back as he struggled, crossing her arms atop his firm buttocks and propping her chin on her hands. Flat on his stomach, arms outspread, and unable to draw up his knees for leverage, Garreth was trapped. "You'll have to get off!" he wheezed after a few moments of futile writhing. "You must be heavier than you look—I can't budge with you on me!"

"Oh, can't you?" That was all the incentive Leara needed. She reached down on either side of him and found his ribs, tickling until he squirmed and roared beneath her.

Finally managing to throw her off, Garreth wasted no time in retaliating. Leara was soon pleading and gasping, begging and making extravagant promises of revenge if he didn't cease and desist at once.

Garreth stopped the torture and rolled off her. He circled her with his arms, pulling her tightly against his chest, and his lips found hers.

"I feel so happy." It wasn't quite the declaration he wanted to make, but it was all he dared for now. Something still kept him from speaking his feelings aloud.

As he looked at her eyes, searching for affirmation that she felt the same happiness, his arms tightened convulsively at the depth of emotion revealed in their clear gray depths.

We'll make it work this time! He told her silently. It had to. She was all he'd ever wanted, and he was over-joyed that he had a second chance.

With a moan, Garreth claimed the sweetness of her lips again, then moved to her throat, his teeth lightly grazing the sensitive skin beneath the point of her jaw as his fingers impatiently fumbled with the buttons of her camp shirt. Her skin flamed everywhere his lips and tongue and teeth touched it.

Leara's heart pounded in her chest, making her whole body throb with its pulsing as she stroked his wide shoulders, relishing the feel of his taut muscles. Garreth's lips were everywhere, his hands slowly slipping over the bare skin of her abdomen as the shirt parted. Almost reverently, his mouth traced a moist path down her tummy. She strained to decipher the unintelligible words he rumbled against her skin. When she could stand no more without kissing him back, Leara caught his face between her palms and forced his head up.

"Garreth!"

Leara couldn't say more. The look darkening his heavy-lashed brown eyes stole her breath away, piercing her with its sweetness. With one gentle finger, she traced the curve of his brow, the line of his nose, wanting never to look away.

"Garreth, I—"

The abrupt ringing of the phone made her start.

"Damn!" Garreth echoed her feelings precisely. Going back to the normally all-consuming task of kissing Leara, he managed to pretend to ignore it for two more rings. "Damn!" he said again, rolling away and plucking the receiver from its cradle.

"Yes? Oh, Teresa—" he grimaced. Leara smiled. "How's everything?"

Propping her chin on her laced fingers as she lay on the bed, Leara watched Garreth as he sat up in the bed and leaned against the headboard. Smiling mischievously, she rolled onto her back, placing her head in his lap. Garreth smiled at her as he listened to what his former sister-in-law was saying, and placed a finger on Leara's lips, drawing an imaginary line down her chin and neck and straight into the vee of her bra. "I'm glad to hear Jenny's okay. Someone's been beeping me and . . .

"What?" Garreth's whole expression changed and he sat bolt upright, his features cold and tense. "No, no—it's okay, but . . ."

A slight frown tugging her brows together, Leara was acutely curious to hear the rest of his side of this conversation. A sudden, imperious knocking at the door thwarted her and she rose to answer it, hastily rebuttoning her blouse on the way. Expecting to find a maid with the extra towels she'd requested earlier, she was thrown off balance as she swung open the door and was confronted by a tall and very beautiful blonde— easily the most striking woman Leara had ever seen.

And a woman whom she recognized at once from her resemblance to Jenny: Jenny's mother, Marlene.

Marlene's hair was a golden nimbus, seemingly layered with light, haloing her flawless face. Her lips were full, her lipstick perfectly applied to create a raspberry cupid's bow. Her blue eyes were at once widely innocent and senuously heavy-lidded. The raspberry jumpsuit she wore showed off her impressive curves perfectly.

One hand on her hip, the other on the door frame, causing the jumpsuit's surplice neckline to gape strategically, the woman had obviously been posed for Garreth to answer the door. When her powder blue gaze fell on Leara, Marlene straightened to her full height, her expression hardening.

"Who are you?" It was a demand.

Leara wet her lips, suddenly very aware of how far she came from measuring up to this goddess.

"I'm—"

"Oh, never mind. I'm sure it's not important. I take it my husband's inside," Marlene said, sweeping past her.

Garreth hung up the phone and rose as Marlene entered, the expression on his face cold. No matter how beautiful Marlene was, he was obviously not pleased to see her.

Or, is it that he's not pleased for Marlene to see him with me? a little voice inside Leara's head asked.

Leara followed her in and closed the door, uncertain of what she should do. Marlene obviously wanted to talk to Garreth, but something ugly had raised its head and looked out of Leara's eyes at the way the blond goddess had referred to Garreth as "my husband." My husband—not my ex-husband, my former husband, my onetime husband—but my husband! Leara had no intention of offering them any privacy!

"Garreth, I—" Marlene paused and looked around at Leara, inviting her to leave. Leara moved beside Garreth. The blond woman's eyebrow rose fractionally as her blue, blue gaze settled in amusement on Leara's blouse. Looking down, Leara realized that in her haste to get to the door she'd buttoned it crookedly. Catching a glimpse of herself in the mirror, she saw to her further chagrin that her hair, always unruly, looked as if it might have been blown dry by a cyclone. She'd obviously been having a tumble in bed.

Casting a resentful glance at Garreth's smoothly composed appearance—why, his hair wasn't even mussed— she felt she looked as if she'd been having it by herself. Leara folded her arms, resisting the urge to smooth her hair, trying to bring order to her dishabille.

With a shrug, Marlene got right to the point. "Garreth, I've arranged a marvelous opportunity for Jennifer! Imagine how she'll love staying in a Scottish castle! It will be like a fairy tale for her, and she'll learn so much! I've been trying to locate you, so that I can make the final arrangements for her to travel with me and—"

"So Teresa told me on the phone," Garreth interrupted. His tone was so cold, Leara looked at him in surprise. He went on, "I'm sorry she told you where to find us. If you'd stayed at the number you gave my answering service until I could reach you, you'd have saved yourself a wasted trip."

"But Garreth! All I want is the two weeks with her that are rightfully mine! I didn't have her the first two weeks in April, as I was supposed to . . ."

"That's hardly my concern. You chose not to take her then. The court's judgment is very specific—"

"I couldn't take her! I'd had emergency surgery!"

Emergency surgery? Her immediate dislike of Marlene was forgotten. Leara had seen too many parents engage in retaliation against their former spouses at the expense of their children.

Leara looked at Garreth in stupefaction—his face was as cold as his voice had been. Every feature proclaimed him inflexible on the matter. Had his marriage truly been hideous enough to warrant this vindictiveness?

No! She shook her head in denial. *No, this is wrong!*

Leara's head swam. Could this be the man to whom she'd been about to confess her love? He was nothing like the man she'd thought him—nothing like the man she remembered . . .

Looking into his eyes, cold and hard and unfeeling, she realized suddenly that she had indeed seen this inflexible side of him. She'd seen that same look in his eyes that night ten years ago when she had begged him to take her away from Columbus.

That realization spurred her to speak up. "Garreth, I know Jenny would want to go with her mother. Time with her mother is very important for a little girl." To Marlene: "She prattles about you constantly."

"Leara," his voice rumbled ominously, "don't step into what you don't understand."

"But, I only—" She stopped. She had argued against that set look once before—argued her heart into shreds—and it hadn't done the least bit of good. "Excuse me."

Leara tried to make an escape. The blond woman reached for and caught her hand as Leara brushed past. "Thank you for trying anyway," Marlene said. She gave Leara a sad smile, moisture apparent in her beautiful eyes. "I don't understand why he hates me. . . ."

Uncomfortable, Leara mumbled something unintelligible and escaped into the hall.

Garreth turned to Marlene, his eyes blazing. He applauded slowly, slapping his hands together like blows. "Bravo!" His sarcasm twisted the word into an insult. "A marvelous performance. Your skills as an actress have dramatically improved." His heart was writhing with the vision of Leara's stricken expression, but his anger at Marlene's selfishness had washed over onto Leara. The thought made him even more angry at his ex-wife. "And tell me, since when is a nose job considered emergency surgery? And what about this wonderful opportunity for Jenny? Just what are you trying to pull now, Marlene?" An answer suddenly occurred to him. "What man are you trying to impress this time?"

He watched the false sincerity cloak her features, her eyes widen, and her perfect brows rise. "Why, it's only that dear Nigel. You remember Lord Rathbane, don't you? Well, Nigel has been kind enough to invite me, and Jenny, of course, to his home in Scotland. His charming daughter will be there on holiday from school, and I was sure that Jenny would adore keeping her company—"

"And show dear Nigel what a loving parent you are, and what a wonderful stepmother you would be for his daughter when you marry," he finished for her. "You have no idea what you did to Jenny when you didn't take her this spring, Marlene. Now, you fly into her life, needing her for your little machinations and you expect me to go along with it. You can find the door."

Leara looked up as Garreth strode into the hotel coffee shop and then back at her untouched coffee.

"You think I was too inflexible with Marlene, don't you?" he asked as he sat down in the chair opposite her.

She did, but she knew she couldn't say so.

"I was trying not to get involved, Garreth. It's really none of my business, is it?"

"I want everything I do to be part of your business. But you aren't aware of the situation, Lea. You don't know what a manipulator Marlene can be." He reached across the table and took her hand in his warm one. "She's always building Jenny up and then letting her down—flying in and out of her life on a whim."

"As long as you're doing it for the right reasons." *And not letting your own bitterness over a failed marriage color your actions,* she added silently.

"I'm only trying to protect Jenny from disappointment."

"But Marlene is Jenny's mother." She couldn't help it. Her heart went out to the woman, although she accepted that Garreth's perceptions might be true. Garreth had never been vengeful.

"I hope to God one day she'll act like it. Until then you'll just have to trust me, Leara." He leaned forward across the table, his brown eyes dark and troubled.

She had to believe that his intentions were good.

TWELVE

Leara smiled a little nervously at Garreth as they entered Kinderland Daycare's northside facility. It was early—a little after seven A.M.—and already sleepy preschoolers were being dropped off by parents on their way to work. Little footsteps rang in the halls; sharp, high-pitched voices and laughter bounced off the walls. The young people were being herded through doors by workers in bright-colored pants and T-shirts. Leara's employees smiled and called hello when they saw Leara and cast curious glances at the tall man who had his arm draped possessively around their boss's shoulders.

As they entered Becky's office, they found her behind her desk, a spreadsheet program displayed on her computer screen. The petite brunette looked up and smiled at the pair in the doorway.

"Hi, Lea. How was the trip?" Leara had called her from Chicago to tell her where to contact her in case of emergency.

"The Cubbies lost—what can I say?" Leara sighed. "Becky Taylor, this big lug is Garreth Conroe."

"Hi. So you're the one who kidnapped Lea." Becky

153

extended her hand. Only as Garreth took it did he notice that she was sitting not in a desk chair but a wheelchair, a modern, low-profile model.

"Actually I plied her with chocolate doughnuts until she was in a glucose stupor, then took advantage of her disorientation."

"Oooo. A hunk like you and doughnuts, too?" Raising a brow, Becky looked at Leara. "And you wasted time at a baseball game?"

Leara was fascinated as the tops of Garreth's ears pinked. The worldly man she'd walked in with suddenly reminded her of a bashful farm boy. "Garreth had the loan of a box behind the Cubbies dugout." She shrugged. "So, any crises shaping up?"

"Only minor. The milk truck hasn't delivered our milk. If it doesn't come by ten, I'm going to send Roberta down to the supermarket. How were the fireworks? I saw a little of them on the late news Saturday night."

"The fireworks?" Leara looked up at Garreth with a secretive smile on her face. "They were spectacular."

"Spectacular," he agreed. The smoky look in his brown eyes made her toes tingle. Neither was talking about the display over Lake Michigan.

"At the risk of mixing a metaphor, I smell an undercurrent," Becky said. "Since you're back, you need to run over to Kramer Street and check on Henderson's crew. I've been calling every fifteen minutes since six A.M.—which is the time he contracted to have his crew on the job. They didn't show up until eight on Friday, remember? We're paying for his crew's overtime, and he's not letting them work it—probably planning to pocket the difference. I don't need to tell you we need to get the center back in operation as soon as possible! That's why we agreed to pay the obscenity-deleted overtime!"

"I know," Leara said and snorted in a most unlady-like manner.

"I'd talked to Henderson about it when they showed up late on Friday, and he just smiled and said—" Becky stuck out her chest, screwed up her face, and huffed in an exaggerated Texas drawl, " 'Doan chew worry none about it, little lady.'

"Luckily there wasn't a two-by-four lying around or I'd have been arrested for assaulting a construction worker."

Leara looked at Garreth. "Do you mind if we go there before you drop me off at my apartment? I want to be there when those jokers arrive!"

"I don't think I'd miss it," he said seriously. Her mouth had formed a straight, determined line. Her gray eyes shot angry sparks. He searched for a trace of the warm, kittenish woman he'd held in his arms a few hours before, but she'd vanished completely.

His Leara had been disappearing a lot lately, but she suddenly reappeared with a dimpled smile. And his heart swelled a little.

Leara clasped Garreth's big hand in hers and tugged him toward the door. "I want to show you around a little before we go on to Kramer Street. See you later, Beck."

As Leara led him through another door, he already heard high-pitched squeals coming from the other side. Then they entered a world of organized chaos. "I guess it's good you're here. They seem to need help," Garreth said.

"This is normal." Leara grinned at his surprised expression. "Kids express themselves in very active ways. They learn by doing, rather than listening, at this age."

"But, it's so . . . noisy. I can't remember it ever being this noisy before eight in the morning."

She led him through the different divisions—infants to four-year-olds—and each room was increasing pandemonium.

She almost laughed when she looked up at Garreth and saw the look on his face—that stunned expression she used to wear when confronted by the noise and the kids' exuberance. She squeezed the hand she still held and led him outside into the sunshine and quiet.

"But what about the little girl wearing only panties and a bowl on her head? Where are her clothes? Shouldn't she be dressed?" he asked, frowning.

"That's Katy. Right now, she has a thing about clothes. We allow kids to express their independence, as long as it doesn't hurt anyone. We've had this happen with others. One of these days soon, when being like others is important to her, she'll decide to wear her clothes again and it'll be all over. Right now, she's asserting her individuality. It loses its appeal really quickly when no one makes a fuss."

Garreth remembered his own upbringing. He had often felt that what he wanted was unimportant. He could remember his dad shushing him at the dinner table when he tried to talk about what he and his friends had been doing. He could remember resenting it.

And he'd been just as blind to Jenny's needs.

"I noticed that there aren't many infants."

"I don't encourage parents of small children to place them in day care for several hours each day. Before the age of one, care by a grandmother, or aunt, or even a steady baby-sitter is much better for the child's emotional development."

"How did you ever come up with this?"

"Many of the ideas came from real innovators in the field. And, like the kids, I learn a lot by doing. I worked for Becky before I became a partner. Becky always had a good staff. But I felt we needed to do more than just care for the kids while their parents were working. They needed activities and stimulation. I started reading books by child care experts. Many of the ideas came from them. And then we hired Theo, and I took some courses at the university—''

"You went to college?"

"I took a few classes. Then I enrolled as a part-time student. It's slow going, but I want to get a degree eventually, probably in child psychology.''

Leara paused to pluck a grass seedling out of a window box filled with bright yellow marigolds. Watching her, Garreth remembered her impersonal apartment—there hadn't been a plant anywhere in sight—and he suddenly understood something that had been puzzling him. The apartment was just a place Leara slept and kept her clean clothes. The day care centers were where her life was.

A few minutes later, they were driving to what had been Kinderland's largest day care center. Leara gave Garreth directions, pointing out interesting places along the way.

"Turn right at the corner. The day care is in the second block.''

Garreth turned and then pulled up to the curb in front of a makeshift plywood fence with a sign that read: KEEP OUT—CONSTRUCTION SITE. Leara got out of the car before he shifted into park. She bounced to the gate and rattled the chain and padlock. No one was inside working.

Leara turned her back to the gate and crossed her arms over her chest, tapping her foot impatiently as she waited to confront the tardy construction crew.

As Garreth joined her, he wondered again where the woman he knew had gone. This was a side of Leara that must have been molded during those lost ten years.

Taking in her determination, he regretted not being there for her during those years, to make her life comfortable and easy, so that this hard-edged woman need never have evolved.

The crew drove up a short time later in a battered crew cab pickup topped with a rusty utility bed on the back and a head rack full of ladders.

"You are late, Mr. Henderson," Leara said to the driver as a flunky got out of the truck and unchained the gate.

"Well, little lady, we had a little trouble getting going—battery was dead, you see—"

"What was wrong Friday?" she asked sweetly, but the look she gave the man could have curdled cream.

"Same thing, missy. Now, we better get—"

"By the way, why did you leave early on Friday?" Leara continued.

One of Henderson's men answered, "Now look here, lady, we put in a full eight hours Friday, just like we got paid for. I don't know what you're whining about but—"

"I'm whining because our contract agrees to pay for four hours a day overtime, to get this job finished quickly, but he seems to be forgetting to let you guys make that extra money. I wonder if he'll forget to include it on his invoice?" she asked acidly.

"Look, lady, I make out the invoices according to the contract." Henderson suddenly lost his good-ole-boy smile. "If you have a problem with that, I can pull my crew off completely. But I guarantee you that no other construction firm this side of the Mississippi will come in and finish our job. Now, will you get that pretty little butt of yours—"

Garreth had stood aside as long as he could. "Pardon me." He stepped in front of Leara, his features coolly composed. Inside he was furious. "My name is Garreth

Conroe. Of Blake, Conroe, and Jeffers, Ltd. You might have seen the name on a few construction sites." A slightly mocking smile curved his lips as he saw the man's face change when the name registered. For added impact, he presented the foreman with his card. "Now, what my fiancée is asking doesn't seem unreasonable to me. After you think about it a few moments, I think you'll agree."

Henderson looked flustered momentarily, then solicitously looked at Leara and agreed that a new battery was in order. And, of course, his invoices would only reflect actual time on the job.

As Leara stepped aside and let the truck through the makeshift gate, she was stunned.

Turning to Garreth, she said incredulously, "You just took over— *Your fiancée*?" She shook her head, marched to Garreth's car, got in, and slammed the door.

"Your fiancée? You haven't asked me! Even if you did, why should I want to marry a man who minimizes my capabilities at every turn?" she asked him scathingly as he slid behind the wheel.

Stony faced, Garreth started the engine and shifted into gear. "You had lost control of the situation—that's why I stepped in," he said stiffly.

"Lost con . . . I knew damned well that Henderson was bluffing. I would have simply told him that I was sorry he felt that way, but he was free to go. Construction jobs are damned hard to come by in this area right now. He would have been calling Becky before we got out of sight!"

Garreth scowled. She was probably right—so why had he jumped in?

"I didn't like the sexist remarks aimed at you!" he gritted out. "It was take over for you, or fight the whole damned crew!"

Leara was quiet for several moments. When she spoke, her voice was calm. And a little sad. "I wasn't surprised by their remarks and attitudes. But I am surprised by yours. Tell me how your attitude is any less sexist?"

Garreth opened his mouth, but he could find no words to dispute what she said.

Folding her arms, Leara sat stiffly on her side of the car for the rest of the way to her apartment.

THIRTEEN

As Leara made her way out of Columbus' new city hall, the July heat hit her like a slap. Heat waves danced off the pavement and the sidewalks in the otherwise still air. Above, flat-bottomed clouds sat like cotton puffs dropped on a glass-topped cocktail table. They were only indicators of the sultry heat, offering no hope of a cooling shower.

A tour bus stopped and a group of sunglassed, middle-aged tourists carrying cameras, cam corders, or straw shoulder bags lethargically got out to view the building Leara had exited.

The brick facade sheltered an imposing curved steel-and-glass entrance. It was only one of Columbus' many eye-catching structures, which were more art than office space, churches, or commercial sites. The North Christian Church and the Indiana Bell Telephone offices and other sites were the main reason the city drew more than sixty thousand tourists each year.

Leara paused and looked back at the graceful structure. The simple elegance of the building and the practicality of the modern, space-aged materials used in its construction seemed to mock her.

She had known before she started that renovating the beautiful turn-of-the-century house on Bartholomew Street and getting it approved as a day care and learning center would be difficult. What she had just discovered was that getting it approved and licensed would be nearly impossible.

The state wanted day care centers to be one-level structures built of modern, flame-retardent materials, such as bricks, cinder blocks, and Sheetrock. There were special requirements for windows, lighting, and ramps to facilitate mobility of the disabled and a host of other regulations, which would have to be met before she could have had the building inspected for licensing. The cost of renovating the house to meet state standards would be too much, and then there were no guarantees that the state wouldn't change the regs in a couple of years, so that the old house would no longer pass inspection.

The state rules and regulations were for the safety of the children—they made sense. Leara's plan to convert the old house into a day care and learning center didn't. It just wasn't practical. Nonetheless, it hurt to let go of her dream.

Why had it been so important to her? Of course, Theo had offered an explanation. He might have been partially right.

"A penny . . . ?" said a deep voice behind her.

Leara gasped in surprise and spun around. Garreth stood there. His tie was loosened. His white shirt was open at the collar and sleeves rolled up to the elbows. Sun glinted off his dark hair and one dark lock had fallen, curling on his forehead. Leara touched his arm, as if assuring herself he was really there. She inhaled the light citrus of his after-shave and wanted to press her cheek to his broad chest and have him wrap those strong arms around her, comforting her as he might a disappointed child—which was exactly how she felt.

"Sorry if I surprised you."

Leara wet her lips with the tip of her tongue. "Why . . . How . . . ?" She looked away and blinked rapidly.

"How did I find you?" She nodded. Garreth chuckled, deliberately trying to lighten her mood. "Marijo is in a quandary, torn between exuberance at the thought of unloading 'that great white elephant of a house'— her words—and a guilty conscience for dumping the elephant atop her best friend. She called me at my office, explained what you were up to, and asked me to come down here and talk you out of it," he said.

He saw her stiffen. Before she could utter the angry comment that he sensed was coming, he continued gently, "I told her there was just one problem with her request: you didn't want, need, or ask my advice. I told her that you're a big girl now. You can cross the street all by yourself. You can make your own decisions, run a business, even decide whether or not a certain property is what you want. In short, whether I like it or not, you're a self-sufficient woman, who doesn't need my sage advice," he added, a rueful smile curving his firm lips.

"It's scorching out here. There's a café down the street. Let's get something cool to drink," he suggested.

Leara nodded.

A few minutes later, Garreth guided Leara inside a quaint little café, which had an old-fashioned soda fountain–type bar complete with brass foot rails and swivel-top bar stools. Huge black and white photos of past movie stars—Bogie, Monroe, James Dean—were displayed on the walls, making the café's distinctive fifties' atmosphere more pronounced.

The café was almost empty. Garreth seated her in a

secluded corner booth and went to the bar to order. When he returned, he had two tall fluted glasses filled with frosty ice cream floats, each topped with a froth of whipped cream, chocolate sprinkles, and a cherry. He placed one in front of Leara and then sat in the seat across from her.

"This looks decadent," Leara murmured. And exactly like what she needed, she added to herself. She took the straw between her lips, sipped, and closed her eyes in appreciation. "Mmmmm."

"So," Garreth said, playing with his straw, "how 'bout those Cubbies?"

Leara laughed and shook her head, causing the coppery curls, which had escaped from the knot at the crown of her head to bounce. "You can talk about it." Her smile faded. "I won't be buying the house."

Garreth made a noncommittal sound, but his warm brown eyes touched her gray ones, briefly, then he returned his attention to his drink. "I'm sorry. You sound like it was important to you."

"When I told Becky about it and what I wanted to do with it, she said that it would be more practical and probably less expensive to build from the ground up. And, as usual where business matters are concerned, she was right. You can't imagine the amount of renovation . . ." Leara paused and drew in a deep breath. "Anyway, Becky's not at all interested in expanding outside of the city of Gary.

"My friend, Theo, was there when Becky and I were talking about it, and Theo—he has a Ph.D. in child psychology—said that my fixation on this antique house was spawned by a subconscious desire for roots and a more stable home life during my early adolescence. Nonetheless, he said everyone deserved to indulge in one neurosis and offered to buy my partnership in the

Gary centers, freeing me to try the project on my own. . . .

"And I've thought about it. Hard. I've explored all the angles. There wouldn't have been quite enough money to buy the old house and make all the renovations I wanted, so I met with a city councilman to explore the possibility of getting the city to finance part or all of the project from its preservation fund. He was enthusiastic and promised to look into it further. But, just now, as I was leaving his office, I realized that even if his answer is yes, I can't go through with it. There are sound reasons behind the guidelines the state has set up for day care centers. Even with extensive renovation, that great old house would never be as safe for the kids as a modern structure designed and built for caring for children. No. You can tell M.J. that I'm not buying."

Leara went on, "When I first saw that house, I made you stop because it was as if it was calling to me. It was as though that house was meant to be mine. And suddenly I was imagining it as children would see it— after it had flower boxes hung from the windows and was painted bright colors. Like a fairy castle . . . I guess Theo's diagnosis was right. When you looked at that house, you saw only the money pit it is." She smiled ruefully. "Still, it is hard . . ." Leara broke off, unable to say more around the sudden knot tightening her throat.

"To let go of a dream?" Garreth finished for her, catching her cold fingers and giving them a sympathetic squeeze.

Leara nodded, wondering how so much heat could be transmitted through such a small amount of contact. The heat tingled as it traveled up her arm, into her chest, and warmed her heart. During their week apart, she'd been examining what she had been substituting for a life and finding it not at all as fulfilling as she had before she'd gone into Ferguson's Market a few weeks ago and come face to face with her past. Her life had mainly consisted of her work. She still loved what she did, but she realized now that she'd been using it to fill the empty areas in the rest of her life. She really hadn't had a life outside her work, other than catching a few Cubbies games and occasional dates with Theo and others like him—men who never quite became more than friends.

"I know," Garreth said quietly. Something in his voice snapped her out of her introspection, alerting her to something wrong. His brows were drawn together, almost touching; his sherry brown eyes were shadowed. He stirred his float with the straw, mixing up the chocolate sprinkles and whipped cream and sinking the cherry, making the concoction look completely unappetizing. Then he looked at her and sighed. "I've been having a hard time letting go of a dream myself. It's why I haven't called you this last week. I've been trying to come to terms with the fact that you're not the same person you were ten years ago, are you? You're not the woman I've been in love with all these years. No." He squeezed her fingers again—this time she felt no warmth—and he shook his head when she started to speak. "Maybe I'm not the same, either."

Leara pulled her fingers free of his grasp, feeling very much as though someone had delivered a blow to her solar plexus. A big part of her disappointment in not getting the Victorian house as a center was that she'd seen it as a way to move back to Columbus, so that she and Garreth could build their relationship again. She knew now that she loved him. She had loved him as a teenager, but she loved the caring, giving man he'd become even more. She listened numbly, barely able to comprehend what Garreth was saying.

"I never stopped caring for you, Leara. Thinking about you—or, rather, the person you were. I guess for ten years I'd imagined you as baking apple pies and sitting around darning socks, and I was damned angry that those socks weren't mine. At the reunion dance, you were so self-assured when you were discussing child care—still, I was surprised when I found out from Robert and Chelsea that you're regarded as something of an expert in the field. I should have seen it then. But I think I had deliberately blinded myself to the changes in you. In Chicago . . . you were magnificent. I've never experienced anything like what you made me feel. You were all woman, not the half-shy girl I'd remembered and expected. When we went to Gary and I saw you at work in your element, I couldn't deny the truth to myself any longer: you are a person in your own right, with a fulfilling career; a strong, self-confident person who gets along perfectly well without my help. You didn't need me like you used to.

"I never stopped caring for you, Leara," Garreth said again, low and earnest, a ragged whisper. "Can you imagine how I felt when I realized that the person I'd been in love with all these years existed only in my memory? And it's not your fault that you've changed. Grown up. I have too. You saw that from the first, didn't you? You've always known that we couldn't go back, and you tried to tell me. I just wouldn't believe you."

Leara swallowed down her rising fear and took his hand in both of hers. "That's why I wanted so much for this project with the old house to work out, Garreth—to be here in Columbus so that we could get to know the people we are now. You see, we wouldn't have made it before—even if you had given in and married me. Our relationship was doomed. It couldn't have lasted. I was too needy. Too dependent. Too insecure. With your strength constantly there to depend on, I would never have grown up and developed any self-confidence. Self-esteem. I would never have developed any strength of my own. After you went to college and your world started expanding, I felt less and less your equal—and more insecure. Even had our relationship lasted through the rest of your college days, as your career started taking off, I would have grown more clinging and demanding, constantly needing reassurance. And you would have grown bored.

"I think I never felt worthy of your love, and always expected to lose you. So, in the end, I unconsciously fulfilled my own expectations."

"Your friend Theo, again?" Garreth asked after a few moments. He felt slightly stunned as he examined her assessment of their past relationship and saw that what she'd said was true.

"Oprah."

Garreth smiled, a slight twisting of his lips. Something about it was so sad, Leara wanted to reach out and smooth it from his face.

"You grew into one wise lady, Leara. You've shown me something about myself," Garreth said. *And about why my marriage to Marlene failed,* he thought. Of course, the main reason was that he'd never really loved Marlene. When he'd married her, he'd honestly believed he'd grow to love her. Strange, when he'd met Marlene, he had thought her completely different from Leara. Marlene was a creature of the spotlight and high society parties. He'd never realized before that what had drawn him to Marlene was that she'd reminded him of Leara—or, rather, the person Leara had been when they'd been in love. . . .

When they'd been in love . . . ?

Garreth shoved his ice cream float aside, untasted,

turned his head, and looked out the plate glass windows, which ran the length of one wall.

"No. There has to be more to what I feel than nostalgia and good sex," he said at length, almost to himself. "There *is* more," he added firmly, turning back to Leara. "You're one beautiful, smart, sexy lady. Since I found you in Ferguson's, I think about you constantly—not about who you were—*about you*—and I want to be with you. And if I met you right now for the first time, I'd be instantly attracted to you. To you, not the person you used to be. And you are probably right about something else—we didn't have a future before. I was too obsessed with living my life according to the plans I had carefully laid out to see your needs.

"I guess that's why we really failed in our relationship. But we might have a future now, if we start fresh. No preconceptions. No old expectations. As if we are meeting for the first time. How about it?"

"I think I'd like that," Leara murmured.

Garreth stuck out his hand. "Hello, I'm Garreth Conroe. And I want to get to know you."

Leara smiled tremulously as his large hand closed over her smaller one. "Hello. I'm Leara Lockwood." Garreth's grip tightened. "What's wrong?"

"Leara James." The lines of Garreth's face were harsh.

Her smiled vanished. Sad gray eyes met fierce brown ones. "Leara James Lockwood. We can't just pretend the last ten years didn't happen. I was married to Quint for eight years, Garreth."

Leara rang Garreth's doorbell. As she waited, she slipped her invitation to Jenny's birthday party out of her purse and smiled as she looked at it again. Inside the card, which had a clown balancing on one finger on the cover, *Jenny* was printed in crayon in odd-sized letters beneath a more adult printing of the time and date. Garreth had added in pen "RSVP"—the sneak! When she'd called to tell him that she'd come, she'd been immediately drafted into helping give the party.

She didn't really mind. In fact, she'd never helped give a birthday party before and she was looking forward to it. Besides, this helped take her mind off her other problems—someone had attempted to torch another of the centers.

Late last Saturday night, a member of the local neighborhood watch had seen someone trying to jimmy open a window at the Klondyke Avenue center. When the police arrived, the culprit ran. The police discovered a can of kerosene and some rags beneath the window.

Leara was bothered most by the description of the suspect: male; twenty-five to thirty years old; medium build; blond hair.

She shook her head. It was easy to leap to conclusions, but it was foolish to think it might be Quint. Arson just wasn't something he was capable of. No, it had to be some nut case.

Which made the whole thing all the more frightening.

Leara tucked the invitation back into her purse and rang the doorbell again. The door opened. "Hi!" Teresa ushered her into the foyer. "I'm glad you could come a little early."

"I'm happy to help out," Leara said. She privately wondered how two sisters could look so much alike and yet be such opposites in personality. Teresa, the younger, seemed to be warm and genuine, even bubbly, while Marlene was all glitz and glamour. Garreth had said Teresa was an excellent assistant. She'd gone to work for him part time when she was still attending the University of Chicago. She'd soon proven a valuable asset to the firm and, after graduation with a B.A. in art, became a full-time employee. She moved with him when he'd moved to Columbus.

Leara might have been jealous of this beautiful, bubbly creature working so closely with Garreth, except for the knowledge that Teresa was safely engaged and happily planning a fall wedding.

Teresa said mournfully, "I'm behind on the party preparations. I was late picking up the cake, and it's gone downhill from there. We're setting it up on the patio. This way." She led the way through the French doors onto a spacious brick patio surrounded by brick planters filled with tiny pompom marigolds. The oaks shading the yard created a cool refuge from the July sun. The whole back yard had been decorated with streamers and balloons. The patio was strung with bright-colored lights that sparkled and winked.

Teresa turned to Leara, "Would you help me set up the games? I'm hopeless with this stuff." She pointed to two large boxes with pieces of equipment sticking out. "There's a bean bag toss and a fishing game. Oh yeah, and here are the horseshoes. Thank goodness they're rubber, or we'd have to board over the windows." As she spoke, Teresa pulled the horseshoe set out of the box and started out on the lawn to set it up.

"Was the carnival theme your idea?" asked Leara as she positioned the bean bag target against the patio wall.

"I think Garreth came up with it. He even hired two clowns to entertain. But he promptly put me in charge of the arrangements and drafted you." Teresa paused and walked over to Leara. "Garreth told me what you said about his relationship with Jenny."

"I don't pretend to be a counselor! I never meant—"

Teresa held up a hand, cutting her off. "I think I sensed something was wrong, too, but it never occurred to me what it was. Anyway, I don't know a great deal about children and parenting. Marlene and I spent most of our time in boarding school.''

Leara smiled ruefully, ''I gave him a pretty hard time about the Teagle.''

''Ah, Jenny insisted on inviting Teagle to her birthday party,'' Teresa said.

''She's here?'' Leara asked. Teresa nodded. ''Where?''

''I didn't think she'd come. She seemed pretty bitter over her sudden dismissal, but she showed up right on time. She's helping Jenny dress right now.''

''I don't know if I can see that woman and not lose my cool over the way she manipulated Jenny!'' Leara snorted.

''You know,'' Teresa lowered her voice conspiratorially, ''I never really liked the woman. She's always reminded me of one of the housemothers we had at Seven Oaks Academy. That woman had a knack for making you feel two inches tall.''

''I'm sure Garreth had no idea that he wasn't giving Jenny everything she needed. Teagle made his household run smoothly and—at the risk of being a female chauvinist—to a man, that usually means all is well,'' Leara said, unaware of the curtain on a nearby bedroom window, which dropped back into place. Leara continued, ''When Garreth and I were dating in high school, I never thought much about his home life. Until one day, out of the blue, he said bitterly how angry and hurt it made him that his father and mother almost never came to his football games. His father was a workaholic, and there was always some business meeting or dinner to go to that was much more important than his children's activities. His mother was the perfect executive's wife, devoting herself wholly to her husband's career. Garreth told me bitterly that whenever his father did ask how a game had gone, his father invariably started talking about his own high school football career. I really think Garreth felt closer to the housekeeper, who looked after him and his sisters, than he did to his parents.''

She looked around at the expensive decorations. "He's trying to be a good parent in the only way he knows—the way his parents showed him—with gifts and parties. It'll take some time for him to learn that just being with him is what's important for his daughter.''

"Speak of the devil . . .'' Teresa tilted her head toward the French doors that led into the dining room of the house. When Leara turned, Garreth was standing in the doorway. He looked completely delicious, his body clad in a black running suit decorated with splashes of red.

Leara's gaze was snagged by a pair of sherry brown eyes. The look in them warmed her and made her aware of just how much she'd missed him during their week apart.

Teresa said, heading back inside, "I'll check and see how Lois is getting along with the punch.''

"You're just in time to help set up the games,'' Leara said as he closed the distance between them.

He pulled her gently into his arms and murmured, "There are games I'd like to play, too.'' His mouth descended slowly. It seemed to take forever. Even while his eyes held her enthralled, she was aware of his warm breath, smelling faintly of mint; of his large slightly rough hand resting softly against her neck. He stopped, his lips nearly touching hers, and he whispered, "Very grown-up games.'' And he kissed her.

She lost herself in the kiss. She could only feel. She felt the softness of his lips, the sharpness of his teeth as her tongue joined his in a battle to expand those feelings. She felt the rush of heat in her body, the pounding of his heart under her hand as it increased its tempo. She felt the throbbing begin low in her belly as he increased the pressure of the kiss, pulled her tighter against his hard length.

A low whistle broke through the fogginess of Leara's brain. Garreth broke the kiss, and she felt as though she were floundering in the sensations that still coursed through her. A mischievous chuckle finally brought her back to earth.

"You guys don't miss a chance, do you?" Marijo said from the doorway. A wide-eyed Kimmi stood beside her.

Kimmi added a cheeky "Nice one, Coach!"

Leara could feel the heat of a blush rush to her face. She had been so lost in the sensations that Garreth's kiss had evoked that she had completely forgotten where she was or that there were people around to see. She was embarrassed to realize that he could have undressed her right there and she wouldn't have resisted.

Leara glanced sideways at Garreth and saw he wasn't the least embarrassed.

"Okay, you two. Kimmi and I are here to help, and a good thing, too. Leara, you should know better than to be unprepared when five-year-olds descend on you. Only large amounts of cake and punch and games can keep them under control. Now, let's get this show on the road. Smoochie smoochie later."

Under M.J.'s ruthless whip, in fifteen minutes the games had all been set up and a large piñata, which M.J. had brought as Jenny's present, hung beneath the patio, sticks with brightly colored ribbons tied to them waiting at the ready.

As Leara looked around, trying to determine if anything else needed attention, nearby, a large rhododendron emitted a distinctive "Psst!" Catching a glimpse of black and red, she smiled and glanced furtively over her shoulder as she ducked behind the bush.

Garreth was waiting. His arms went around her. "Now, where were we—ah, I remember," he murmured and kissed her temples, her eyes, the top of her ear, while smoothing his hand tantalizingly up and down her back. "I've missed you so much this week. I've thought about you a million times. And about this . . ." His kiss was deep and unhurried. It led to other kisses.

"So there you shirkers are!"

Both groaned and looked up to find M.J. tapping her foot impatiently, arms crossed over her ample chest. "Two kids have already arrived. Kimmi's entertaining them, but more are on their way. Back to work."

Teresa and the maid had begun setting the picnic table with little cherry-red and lemon-yellow boxes tied with ribbon, presents for Jenny's guests. Leara placed the paper plates and plastic forks and party favors. A soft breeze stirred the leaves of the trees and made the streamers dance. It also made the paper table cloth billow and sail until M.J. solved the problem by placing cups filled with punch on the corners.

As Leara worked, she watched Garreth as he surveyed the scene, obviously looking for what he could do to help. His eyes were bright with enthusiasm. Why, you'd think it was his birthday party! Leara thought with a smile. Then his gaze found hers and she felt a consuming warmth. Joy. With this man was where she wanted to be, always—and it was time she stopped denying it.

"Leara! Leara!" A tiny blond sprite ran to her, hugging her tightly around the knees, and her joy was complete. "Look at my new dress!" Jenny exclaimed and danced around in a circle, holding her full skirt out to the side for Leara to see. The dress was a confection of ruffles and lace in a bright sunny yellow. "My mommy bought it 'specially for my birthday—isn't it the most beautifulest dress in the world?''

"Why, it is! I've never seen a more beautiful dress!" Jenny's brown eyes danced with delight at Leara's compliment.

"Yes, indeed!" chirped an older lady from the doorway. Leara decided she must be the Teagle. "You will undoubtedly be the most beautiful little girl at your party. Quite fitting, I'd say."

Garreth made introductions. As Leara shook hands, she saw a look of dislike cross the Englishwoman's face.

"Are you planning to return to England?" Leara asked smoothly.

"Eventually, I suppose. I'm in no hurry. I've long kept a little house on the west side of town, where I'd get away to on my off days. Excuse me. I'll just pop in the kitchen and see if Lois needs a bit of help." Teagle nodded to Garreth. "With your permission, of course?"

"Fine, Grace."

There was an insistent tugging at the hem of Leara's blouse. "Yes, Jenny?" she asked, squatting down to the child's level.

"Know what?" Jenny said excitedly. "Mommy's coming to my party! She is! She called me on the phone and told me. Mommy said she loves parties and this is gonna be the best party ever!"

Leara saw a look of disapproval cross Garreth's face, to be immediately replaced by a tender smile as his daughter bounced up to him to show off her dress. Leara hoped his problems with his ex-wife wouldn't put a damper on Jenny's happy day.

More children arrived, and Leara became busy officiating as they played games. The prizes were simple carnival giveaways, like finger pullers, plastic whistles, and tiny stuffed animals. Every child won a prize, and the excitement and laughter added to the carnival atmosphere. When the clowns arrived, the children gathered around while they made balloon animals and did magic tricks.

Leara was taking a much-needed break, sitting next to Teresa on the picnic-table bench, when she realized that Jenny wasn't in the crowd of children around the clowns.

Garreth had gone inside a little while before. Perhaps Jenny had gone inside to find him, Leara thought. She walked to the doors and was about to go into the house when she spotted a flash of yellow in the corner of the patio, behind a huge fern. Going around the large planter, she found Jenny sitting on the bricks, tears running down her cheeks and her shoulders shaking with gulping sobs.

FOURTEEN

"Jenny! What is it?" Leara knelt. Sitting on the bricks beside her, she pulled Jenny onto her lap. Jenny's tiny arms went around Leara's neck and she broke into fresh sobs, her little body trembling.

Leara murmured soothing sounds and rubbed the child's back to try to calm her. When the sobs had subsided somewhat, she said very gently, "Jenny, what happened? Maybe I can help."

There was a long silence as Leara waited for her to speak. Against Leara's shoulder, in between the hiccuping sobs, Jenny told her, "I waited and waited and waited. Mommy's not going to come. She's not going to come and I wanted her to so much!"

"She might just be late," Leara offered, her heart aching with the depth of the little girl's misery.

Jenny shook her head fiercely. "I asked Daddy when she was coming. He didn't know. So, I waited and waited, then I asked Daddy again, and Daddy called her. I heard Daddy on the phone. He was real mad. He was arguing with Mommy, 'cause she's not gonna come."

179

Leara raised Jenny's face and looked into her tear-swollen eyes. Her little voice was filled with pain as she continued, "Mommy promised she would—she promised!"

Her golden head bowed as a flood of fresh tears streamed down her cheeks. She sat slumped in Leara's lap, her shoulders shaking as she cried noisily.

Leara's heart went out to the child, even as she felt a breathtaking surge of anger at the child's mother. Jenny was a beautiful, sunny, delightful little person— what kind of mother could ever disappoint her so callously?

If she was mine . . . The thought jumped into Leara's mind, unbidden. She suddenly realized why Garreth had been so hard with Marlene in Chicago. No doubt, this wasn't the first time Marlene had let Jenny down.

Shaking off her anger at Marlene, Leara concentrated on Jenny's pain. "Honey, it's all right to be mad at your mommy—go ahead, be mad! Be as mad as you want! She should have kept her promise. I don't know why she didn't come to your party—but it's not because of something you did wrong. It's not your fault, understand? It's okay to be angry—cry all you want to.

"You know," Leara went on, rocking the child gently, "I don't know how anyone could miss *your* birthday party. You are so very special! Very, *very* special! The only Jenny Conroe—did you know that? Even if some other little girl has the same name, no one else has *this* little heart," Leara said, placing her hand on the child's heart and feeling its rapid beating. "And no one else has these beautiful eyes. And no one else sees the world exactly as you do! And no one else laughs Jenny Conroe's laugh or smiles Jenny's smile. Why, you're magic! One of a kind! And incredibly special and precious.

"Your mommy should have come to your party. But, it's not *your* fault that she didn't. It's not because there's anything wrong with you. You are a *special, special* little girl."

Jenny's face revealed her doubt. "But maybe if I was very, very good—"

"But you *are* very, *very* good!" Leara exclaimed. "Look at all the people who *did* come to your party," she said. "Look at how many people love you exactly as you are!"

Leara wiped at the little girl's tear-stained faced with a paper napkin, then gave it to her and instructed her to blow her nose.

Jenny obeyed, then her large brown eyes searched Leara's face. "Does everyone here love me?"

Leara smiled. "Oh yes! Very, *very* much!" She hugged Jenny and placed a soft kiss on her forehead.

Jenny's brown eyes, so like her father's, opened wide. Her mouth curved in a smile and the sparkle that Leara had seen earlier returned. In seconds, Jenny had slipped from her lap and rejoined the other children, who were marveling at the acrobatics of the clowns.

Leara was watching Jenny when she felt a prickle at the back of her neck. She looked up to find Garreth, his face etched with tenderness as he watched her through the long window.

Garreth's chest felt tight. Powerful emotion clenched his heart. He had ended his pointless argument with Marlene and gone to find his daughter and soothe her disappointment. As he'd passed by the window looking out onto the patio, the sight of Leara hiding behind the planter with Jenny had stopped him.

He might have soothed Jenny by telling her that her mother loved her very much and really wanted to be here. He would have told her lies to soothe the pain of her disappointment. And then the next time Marlene had let Jenny down, not knowing what else to do, he would have lied again.

Leara had always been a giving person, but what she had just given Jenny was priceless—the knowledge that she deserved to be loved just for herself. Leara had reassured Jenny that there was nothing wrong with her to cause her mother not to love her. And had given her permission to be angry—without feeling guilty for it—with her mother for letting her down.

His eyes filled with unexpected tears. Leara was so special. Impossibly, he loved her more now then before—a new love, growing in the ashes of the old, and holding the possibility of a wonderful future.

Garreth went outside. He found Leara brushing off the seat of her pants.

"Thank you for what you said to Jenny."

She smiled and touched his cheek. "I'm sorry. In Chicago, I didn't think you were being fair to Jenny in not letting her go to Scotland with her mother. I know—you explained your reasons. But I guess I've seen a lot of divorced parents indulge in petty vindictiveness at the expense of their children, and even though you told me that Marlene was likely to get Jenny's hopes up about the trip and then let her down by not taking her, I guess I really didn't believe it. I see now why you reacted the way you did to Marlene's *marvelous* plan."

Garreth laced his long fingers through hers and kissed her knuckles. "Come on. I see everyone's heading for M.J.'s piñata."

"Still thinking about the birthday party?" Leara called as Garreth, after having swum the length of Tarzan's Lake twice, started on his third time.

He cut the lap short and paddled over to where she

treaded water near the center. "Marlene's callousness is still burning me up," he admitted.

"You aren't responsible for your ex-wife's actions."

"Oh, no? I could have seen how she was and never married her."

"Then you wouldn't have Jenny."

"Point taken," he grinned and stole a damp kiss. "I like that swimsuit."

"I bet you do," she groused good-naturedly. When Garreth had suggested swimming, she'd made him take her by Gram's, where she remembered seeing this suit in her old things. The red bikini was very out of style compared to modern, form-fitting spandex suits, and unlike when she'd bought it years ago, the top half barely contained her. She kept checking to make sure she hadn't burst a seam or popped out of it.

"I still feel guilty for slipping out after the birthday party and leaving Teresa and Lois to clean up," she said.

"We could go back," Garreth said, moving closer and sliding his leg sensually between hers underwater as they both treaded water. "Or . . ."

Suddenly, he was against her, an arm around her waist. Their legs moved in unison to keep them afloat. The feel of his water-slick body, the coolness of the water, the heat of his skin, were unbelievable. She could barely breathe with the force of the emotions suddenly flaming through her. Anticipation of his kiss raced through her body, settling low in her abdomen as a hungry ache. Slowly, his mouth possessed hers in an all-consuming kiss, and she thought, surrounded by water as they were, she would burst into flame. His mouth was a molten cavern that she explored with her tongue. She gasped at the desire that sang through her when he nipped gently at her lower lip. He nibbled at her chin, then her throat, flicking at her skin with his

tongue to soothe the bites. When his hands cupped her
buttocks, pulling her against his hips in a hungry gesture, they sank beneath the sun-warmed water of the
pond.

They both resurfaced simultaneously. "Do you want
to swim to shore, or stay here and risk drowning?"
Garreth asked, cupping her breast through the red cotton of her suit.

"Shore," she gasped, arching with pleasure as his
thumb found the tight bud of her nipple through the red
cotton.

Garreth swam backwards, pulling Leara with him,
holding her hands in his as he used his powerful legs
to propel them across the pond.

Sometime later, Garreth rolled onto his side and
propped himself on an elbow. He gazed down at Leara
with a musing smile curving his mouth. Her face was
flushed with their lovemaking, tiny damp tendrils curling around her face. Her eyes were closed, and the skin
of her eyelids looked translucent above her lashes. He
took in every detail of her: the inner curve of her ear,
the slight flaring of her nostrils, the soft curve of her
breast where it rested against her arm.

He loved the way she responded to him, even in
sleep. He lightly caressed her breast and smiled as her
areola crinkled and her nipple elongated at the touch.
Her lips parted when he blew a gentle stream of air
over them. She was everything he had ever wanted in
a woman. No, that was wrong. She was Leara. She
was all that was female in his mind. All that was love
in his heart.

Leara's eyes opened slowly, and his heart constricted
when he saw the way they lighted at the sight of him.
"Hello, sleepyhead," he murmured. He dropped a light
kiss on her warm lips. "Did you have sweet dreams?"

"No dream could be sweeter than this." She reached out and smoothed his hair back from his forehead.

Garreth smiled and held his closed hand out to her. She pried open his fingers to find a small white stone in his hand. It was in the shape of a heart. She looked up into his eyes.

"This is a new keepsake," he said. "For a new dream."

FIFTEEN

"The sunset was beautiful," Leara said. Garreth's arm was draped over her shoulder as they walked to the door of his home. He stopped in the entry porch and turned her to face him.

"Not as beautiful as you were in the orange light. You looked like some sort of witch."

"A witch? I like that!" She punched his arm.

"You cast a spell over me." His tone implied more than just magic. He waved his hands in the air, casting a mock spell. "It doesn't work for me," he teased.

"Oh, you have your moments." She was sliding her hands up his chest when the door opened.

"Daddy! I heard your car! Why are you still outside?" Jenny hurled herself at Garreth, crowding Leara away from her father. "I asked Mrs. Teagle to stay and have supper with us. Is that okay, Daddy? Why isn't she my nanny anymore? Did you tell her to go away?"

Leara looked up to see the older woman standing in the doorway, purse in hand.

"Now, now, Jenny! You do ask a lot of questions, don't you, dear?" Teagle said, coming forward. To

Garreth, she explained, "I was just leaving. After the party, Jenny asked me to stay for a bit, and I thought you shouldn't mind—I *am* very attached to this little girl, you know." Mrs. Teagle smiled down on her former charge and smoothed her golden curls.

"Where is Kimmi?" Garreth asked, frowning.

"Fell asleep on the sofa over some homework for a summer school class she's taking. Well, I'm off," Teagle said.

Jenny turned her attention to the nanny. "But I want you to stay! Don't you want to be my nanny anymore?"

"Now, Jenny," Garreth said, going down on one knee to look his daughter in the eyes, "I've explained to you that you're going to go to nursery school, as soon as there is an opening."

"I don't wanna go to nursie school! I want Mrs. Teagle to stay!" Jenny started to cry.

Leara said, kneeling, "Some things just have to be. Nursery school—"

"I don't want to go to nursie school! Go away!" Jenny told Leara, crying all the harder. "Go away! Make her go away, Daddy!"

"Children naturally get very attached to their nannies, and it's always a wrench to let go. She might calm down if I leave—good-bye, Mr. Conroe. Mrs. James." The nanny started for her car, which was parked at the curb.

"Don't go! Don't go! Please don't . . . !" Jenny screamed.

Shaking her head, Mrs. Teagle got into her car and drove away.

The little girl's cries for her nanny ended in shaking sobs, which tore at Leara's heart. But she reminded herself that the woman had to go—she had not provided Jenny with the quality care she needed and deserved.

She tried to take Jenny in her arms, but the child pushed her frantically away. "You! You go away!"

Garreth turned his daughter to him, and she wrapped her arms around his neck. "Munchkin, why are you—"

"I don't want her here!" She turned back to Leara. "Go a-way!" She made a pushing motion as if she'd physically shove Leara back. "I want Mrs. Teagle. And I want my mommy!"

Leara frowned and stood up. She made a negating gesture to Garreth, but she was more upset than she wanted him to know.

Garreth stood, carrying his daughter with him, her arms wrapped firmly around his neck, as if afraid to let go.

He looked helplessly at Leara. "I wanted to spend some time with you. Have you spend time with us both. You and Jenny seemed to be getting along so well, I really don't understand this. . . ."

"She's had a tiring day. In some ways, a disappointing day. And she *is* attached to her nanny. It's natural for her to be upset—she probably only now realized that Mrs. Teagle is going away for good."

"She's not! You go away!"

Leara blinked back tears. "We've all had a long day, and I really should be getting back to Gram's, anyway."

"Okay, Lea. Lunch tomorrow, then? I have a meeting in the morning, but if you could meet me at Castle's Restaurant about noon, the rest of the day could be ours."

"Okay." Leara was still frowning over the abrupt change in Jenny. She wondered if, because Jenny had an absentee mother, the little girl had looked on the nanny as a substitute. That would make the Englishwoman's methods all the more reprehensible.

Garreth shifted his small burden and leaned forward to give Leara a short, warm kiss.

*   *   *

Leara slid into a back booth in Castle's Restaurant. It was ten until twelve. She was early, but her morning had been a series of restless twistings and turnings. Her afternoon with Garreth at the lake yesterday had been a sweet beginning. Even though they had made love in Chicago, reality had soon put all the questions back into her mind. But their time at that place in the woods had renewed the magic. Then Jenny's rejection had put a damper on her happiness, but she had to believe the child didn't mean what she had said. She'd just been tired and upset that her mother didn't show.

Digging in her purse, Leara brought out the heart-shaped piece of frosted quartz that Garreth had given her. His finding it had been the final connection between the young couple of ten years ago and the one of today. Could they really make it work this time?

"That's very pretty." The comment came from the pretty brown-haired waitress. Puzzled for a moment, thinking that she'd seen the woman before, Leara finally recognized her as Quint's date at the reunion dance.

"Thank you, Fran. Yes, it is. It was a gift from someone very special." Smiling, she tucked the stone back into her purse. "How have you been?"

"Fine. I guess you haven't seen Quint? He said he was going out of town for a few days, but he'd be back today."

Leara saw an open question in the other woman's face. After what Quint had pulled at the dance, Leara could understand if the woman was feeling insecure where she was concerned. She could think of nothing she could say to put Fran at ease.

She'd almost called Garreth last evening and changed their meeting place when she remembered that Fran worked here. But she had changed her mind. After all, if she was serious about coming here to Columbus, she wouldn't avoid places just because her ex-husband might show up.

"Why, no. I haven't. Not for quite a while. Nor do I expect to. He and I don't socialize," Leara said, but her mind had snagged on the fact that Quint had been out of town at the same time as the second attempt at arson.

Leara didn't like what she was thinking. It had to be coincidence—arson was not Quint's style.

She sighed. She owed it to Quint to talk to him about it before she told the Gary police that his description fit that of the man seen trying to torch the Klondyke Avenue facility.

"What can I get you?" Fran was all business now, her order pad and pencil poised.

"Oh, just a coffee. I'm a bit early. I'm meeting someone."

Fran brought her the coffee, and Leara settled into the corner of her seat, her mind going over all the hitches in her plans for the umpteenth time.

The Victorian house was out. She knew that. But part of her still wanted it. The dream of a learning center would have to be put away, at least for the time being. A new day care center would take all the money she would get from her share of the Gary partnership.

Did that mean she had decided to move back home? The prospect was frightening. Oh, she had confidence enough in the success of a business here, but what if she and Garreth didn't work out? Could she handle seeing him go on with his life here without her? Would she be able to live in Columbus if they became memories again—painful memories?

So many questions. So little was certain.

"You sure are intent on your thoughts, darlin'."

Frowning in displeasure, Leara looked up at Quint. "Fran said that you were out of town. What—"

"I just got back and I always eat lunch here." He slid into the booth facing her, his hands clasped. His blue eyes stared into hers. "You look hungry. How about a burger with your coffee?"

"I'm not ready to eat yet," Leara stated. She looked up to see Fran glaring at her from near the lunch counter. Couldn't he see the woman was crazy about him?

"I guess I can wait, too." He sat back, a self-satisfied grin on his face.

"You should be talking with Fran."

She tilted her head toward the sullen waitress who was watching his every move intently. "I guess you've been too busy to call her."

He didn't even have the grace to look embarrassed. "I've been out of town for a few days. A little finance training course in Chicago. I just got back this morning."

Chicago? Gary was only a short drive from the city. Again she could hear the description of the man seen trying to pry a window open at the center— "medium height, blond hair."

No. It couldn't be. Why? Why would he? Revenge?

Leara shook her head, looking into Quint's face. His bright blue eyes were friendly, if a little hungry. It didn't make sense. Even if he'd thought of it, he'd never risk it. Still, she had to ask the question, then she'd know for certain. She'd always been able to tell when Quint wasn't telling the truth. "Quint—"

There was a step nearby. "Lockwood." Garreth's voice was a growl. His eyes, when he turned them to Leara, were dark and forbidding. "Leara."

Quint smiled at Garreth. "Hello, Conroe. Join us?"

"Hardly," Garreth said. The single word held a

definite warning. "My lunch with Leara is intended to be private."

"Oh, really? Sorry, Conroe." Quint smiled at Leara. "You should have told me you already had a lunch date."

Wonderful! Leara thought. *He's made it sound like I wanted him to sit here.* She could see in Garreth's face that his mind had moved in that direction.

"Maybe you can charm Fran into sharing your meal with you," Leara countered. The waitress's face was suddenly sporting a pleased smile. Quint rose, gave them a nod, and headed for a distant booth. Fran trailed in his wake.

"How do you always manage to end up with Lockwood in attendance?" By the time he was seated across from her, Garreth's expression had lightened a bit, but a cloud of doubt still shadowed his brown eyes.

"He invited himself." She was a little irritated that he expected an explanation. After all, he was the one who had asked for her trust.

"I wish he'd get the message that you two are divorced and that he no longer has a proprietary right to your time." His words were clipped with anger.

"Garreth." She paused, waiting until he looked into her eyes. "Quint is harmless." She felt a sudden chill as the arson again crossed her mind. She couldn't mention it to Garreth. Not now. "He thinks he's being charming, flirting. As long as it doesn't mean anything to me . . ."

Garreth watched her face. She had to know what it did to him, still, to see her with her ex-husband. He felt ashamed of the jealousy that filled him, almost choked him whenever he saw them, but he couldn't help it. And it didn't help at all that she was defending Quint to him.

He took a long breath and forced himself to relax.

He leaned across the table and took her hand. "Let's order lunch. Then we can decide what to do with our afternoon."

When the burgers had been placed before them, Leara asked, "How was Jenny this morning?" She poured ketchup over her fries, studiously being casual.

"I don't know. I mentioned at breakfast that we'd be spending the afternoon with you, and she started pouting again. I've never seen her do that before." His straight brows drew together in a frown. "I thought she had recovered from her disappointment with her mother. Maybe she's feeling she's being disloyal to her mother if she likes you too much." He took a bite of his cheeseburger.

"Maybe." Leara was doubtful of that analysis. Kids Jenny's age didn't usually have any trouble making the distinction between friends and family. But what if she was aware of Garreth's feelings for Leara? Could Jenny be jealous?

She wished that she was a little farther along in her counseling courses. She'd been taking night courses, interspersed with a few hours a week at a local college, but because of her heavy work schedule, she was still thirteen college hours away from her B.S. and years away from her master's in psychology.

Her instincts told her that the shift in Jenny's feeling toward her was too dramatic, too sudden not to signal something serious—but what could have caused it? She decided to call Theo. His work with disturbed children had won national recognition.

"Everything will work out," Leara told him, sensing he needed reassurance.

"You're probably right. Maybe she'll be better this afternoon. There are boat races at the lake north of town—I know she'd enjoy it. How about you?"

"I would like that. We can try."

"The races start about two." A teasing grin twisted his lips. "If you can keep your hands off me for that long."

"You—!" Leara threw a french fry at him. His chuckle was infuriating and contagious. "I don't think my hands are the problem!"

Garreth pulled his car to a halt in front of Leara's grandmother's house. "Thank you for today, Lea. I know it wasn't everything we wanted, but you never allowed my mood or Jenny's bad behavior to affect you." His voice was soothing.

"I didn't do anything, really. Jenny's behavior upset both of us. Maybe I should have—"

"Given in and left?" Garreth cut in. "I don't think that would have helped, do you?"

Leara shook her head. She was miserable that Jenny had been so upset.

"Look, Leara, when we went to pick Jenny up to take her to the boat races, neither one of us expected her to throw a fit, but then she's never had to share me with anyone, not that she can remember. Maybe it's just jealousy."

"But she acted like she was afraid of me, too. It kills me to think that something about me is causing her pain."

"She's not the only one in pain," Garreth murmured. He pulled Leara into his arms and held her close. "We'll get to the bottom of the problem. I really think it will pass when she has time to get used to the idea of the three of us being together."

Leara pulled away from Garreth's comforting arms. "I hope so. I keep remembering the way Jenny reacted. And something else has been nagging at me. The look on Teagle's face when Jenny started crying yesterday. It was almost . . . smug."

"You don't think Teagle was filling Jenny's head with nonsense, or frightening her, do you? Why that . . ."

"We don't know that that's what happened. She might have nothing to do with this." She laid a staying hand on his arm, feeling the tense muscles under her fingers. "It's most likely as you said: Jenny's probably just reacting to the amount of time you and I are spending together. I have to go back to Gary tomorrow, anyway. Let's just put us on the back burner for the week. Maybe if Jenny sees that I'm not going to take you away from her, she'll relax." She moved toward him along the car seat. "It's still early enough for you to tuck her in. Why don't you go on home?"

He reached up and caressed her cheek. "You're right. But I was hoping to tuck you in."

Leara smiled. "I'll miss you. Call me tomorrow night?"

SIXTEEN

Leara placed the chicken salad sandwiches she'd made in the wicker picnic basket, looked around Gram's small kitchen, and spied bags of cookies and potato chips on the old table.

Not the best in nutrition, she decided as she added them to the contents of the basket. She tossed in a package of paper napkins and glanced at her watch. Good—she had plenty of time to slip into her new swimsuit before Garreth came to pick her up. It seemed like an eternity since they'd been together—not just last weekend.

They were going to spend the day at a local lake, water-skiing and picnicking. And she couldn't wait to see him. She hoped Jenny would be coming, too.

Leara sighed, but a smile curved her lips as she moved to her old bedroom. A smile that had nothing to do with the scrap of chocolate-brown spandex that lay on the bed, daring her to be daring.

It had happened.

Though she had unconsciously fought against it—and she recognized now that she *had* fought against it—it had happened. Just as some deep part of her sensed it would the very instant—that wonderful and frightening instant—when she'd first seen Garreth in Ferguson's Market.

Garreth had become completely necessary in her life.

Again.

And she was happy about it.

She needed his smile, his companionship, but most of all his love. Perhaps she always had. She had simply shoved her feelings for him so far down, she had been able to pretend she was happy with her life just as it was. She'd had a certain contentment, but that contentment had been a diet salad; the happiness she felt now was a steak and potatoes meal.

Leara knew now that she wanted to share her life with him, and their love would be the most beautiful part of that life.

Two things would make her happiness complete. The first would be when Jenny accepted her. Leara had talked about it with Theo, but he hadn't thought it was a matter for concern, as long as none of Jenny's other behavior patterns underwent sudden, dramatic changes. He had offered a vague "Give it time, but don't let it rule what you and Garreth do."

The second thing was for Garreth to say the words "I love you."

She was just being silly, she knew. Hadn't he said it with his eyes, his body, his caring? But she wanted to hear the three words from him once again—it had been ten years since she'd heard them.

Perhaps those three words would come when she told Garreth what she'd gone to see Theo about—to accept his offer to buy out her partnership with Becky.

She was coming home.

Leara's eyes widened as she studied her swimsuited reflection in the slightly foggy mirror on the back of the door. The saleswoman had assured her the suit flattered her femininity. Seeing the way the spandex hugged her full breasts and the French-cut legs exposed her pelvic bones, she knew the woman hadn't lied. And the color set off her copper curls. The question was, did she really have the nerve to wear it? After all, there'd be more people at the lake than just Garreth, who'd love it, and Jenny, who wouldn't notice it.

She hoped Garreth could convince Jenny to come; however, she'd asked Garreth not to force or manipulate her, but to let the child make her own decision.

Leara sighed. This problem with Jenny was taking some of the shine off her joy. She really wanted Jenny to realize that she wasn't a threat to her. Her and Garreth's love would only create a happy, stable environment for his daughter; it wouldn't take any of Garreth's attention and affection from her.

Right now, the little girl seemed to be angry with Leara and blaming her for Mrs. Teagle's departure. Theo had agreed with her that it was only natural for the child to be strongly attached to the woman, in light of her absentee mother, and the quality of the care the woman had given Jenny had little to do with the bond the child felt. It would just take time and patience to win Jenny's trust.

Leara was glad Chelsea had helped Garreth place Jenny in a good nursery school. Half a day of uninhibited play with other children would do her a world of good.

A pounding at the door interrupted her thoughts.

"Be there in a second!" Leara called. Garreth and Jenny were early—at least, she hoped Jenny had agreed to come with him.

Giving the swimsuit one last doubtful glance, she decided it should be a surprise and threw on her old chenille robe to hide it before rushing to open the front door.

"Quint!" Leara felt a wave of disappointment wash over her that stripped the smile from her lips. "What are you doing here?"

"Bringing doughnuts." He smiled brazenly and hefted the box he carried for emphasis, then brushing past her, just as if she had invited him in. "Good morning, sweetheart."

"I've always wanted to ask: do you work at being annoying, or is it simply a gift?" Leara still held the door open, silently inviting him to exit the same way he came in.

"Don't look at *me* that way, sweetheart. It was you who called me and asked me to come by, remember? Last night? You left a message on my machine."

Leara groaned as she did remember, closed the door, and pulled her robe together at the collar as she noticed the direction of his gaze.

"Quint, you're impossible! You know all I said was that I needed to meet with you, and because I'm staying at Gram's and there's no phone, I'd call you back."

She wanted to ask him face to face if he'd been the one to set fire to the Kramer Street center and if he'd tried to torch the other one. She'd always been able to look into Quint's eyes and know when he was lying and when he was telling the truth.

"Sounded like an open invitation to me, sweetheart," he chuckled as he helped himself to a Styrofoam cup from a stack by the percolator she'd brought with her from Gary. He poured himself a cup of coffee. "There's some chocolate creme-filled."

"I'm not hungry, thank you." She sat down at the table and he took a seat across from her in the only other chair.

"I did want to talk to you, Quint." Since he was

here, she might as well get it over with, she reasoned. "You knew someone had set fire to one of the Kinderland centers in Gary. Well, someone tried to torch another one last week. Only, this time there was a witness." She paused for emphasis, watching his eyes closely. She had his full attention. "The arsonist's description fits you to a T. Why did you do it, Quint?"

He coughed, almost choking on the bite of doughnut he'd been in the process of swallowing. *"Lea!"* He squeaked, then was seized by another bout of coughing. "Lea, I didn't know about any of this—how can you even *think* it!"

Leara smiled, relieved it wasn't Quint. Quint never lost his poise when telling a lie. And there was a certain timbre in his voice that always betrayed him to her. He was obviously innocent.

"The first fire was the night of the dance. You were mad as hell because I was with Garreth. Then the attempt at arson last week when you were out of town, and the man's description . . . well, you can see why I had to ask."

"I was mad, Lea, at the dance. But I spent the night with Fran."

"She's a nice person—" Leara stole a glance at her watch, "—and I think she's crazy about you."

"Are you going somewhere?" he asked casually, his eyes traveling to the front of her swimsuit, revealed as the neckline of her robe gaped open. "Nice swimsuit, by the way. It makes you look like you're smuggling grapefruits. That should drive Conroe to distraction— would you like me to disappear before he comes to pick you up?" He grinned audaciously as he rose.

"Please," Leara bit out, not bothering to deny that Garreth was coming. She rose, too, clutching the front of her robe tightly together, and saw him out the door.

Quint paused on the open porch, gazing up the street. Leara saw a sly smile cross his face.

"Quint, what are—!"

Whatever else she might have said was cut off as Quint turned suddenly, catching her to him, and his mouth came down hard on hers. He held her roughly, kissing her passionately, bending her slightly backward over one arm. He locked his fingers in her sleep-tousled curls to hold her head still.

Leara writhed against him, trying desperately to push him away. He held her immobile by trapping one of her hands between them and catching the other with the arm he had wrapped around her as he'd bent her back.

Outraged, Leara wriggled and strained until she'd freed the hand he'd trapped between their bodies. She wound her fingers into his hair, pulling with all her strength. It had the desired effect as he broke the kiss.

"Yeow! Lea!" Quint yelled in pain. "Stop pulling my hair!" But he still held her to him. "Lea! I didn't hurt any—yeow!" He was forced to release his hold on her completely and, grabbing her hand with both of his, pried her clutched fingers out of his hair.

Suddenly, she was no longer off balance and Quint yelped again as the palm of her hand forcefully connected with his cheek.

"Ouch! Okay! Okay! You've made your point! You know I love you. I just thought some of the old fire—" He rubbed his cheek.

"Get away from me and never—*never*!—touch me again, or I will bring charges!" Leara was heaving for breath, her anger all-consuming. "For *years* I've felt guilty because I married you and I didn't love you. I used your love—I was young and angry, but that's no excuse. I've felt guilty for causing your pain, because you loved me so much, you said, and I never could love you. *No more!* Now, you have someone who cares deeply for you, and you are stringing Fran along, using her—''

''I don't love Fran, Leara! You know I've always loved—''

''I *don't* love you, Quint!'' Leara interrupted. ''Just like you don't love Fran. Go on with your life, and leave mine *the hell* alone!''

Leara slammed the door resoundingly and leaned against it.

Garreth guided the Mercedes through the traffic, unaware of anything but the turmoil in his mind.

Leara. And Quint.

He could still see the passionate embrace, Leara moving against Quint's body, her hand tangled in the man's blond hair. The slit in her robe showing a naked leg and thigh—*No!*

His mind wouldn't accept it. His heart felt like a ball of fire in his chest. He could hardly breathe.

The blaring of a horn brought him back to the street. A driver passed by in the opposite lane, shaking his fist, obviously cursing at him. Shaking, Garreth pulled his car over in the next open space along the curb.

Garreth put his head down on the hands clutching the steering wheel like a lifeline. He couldn't think. All he could do was feel. The scene replayed on his closed eyelids. Leara, her hair still tousled from sleep, in Quint's arms, locked in a kiss that lasted for eternal seconds. Obviously, still caught up in the passion after a night spent in each others arms.

The heat in his chest became a brand, burning away all his dreams. Suddenly, all that was left was rage.

Lockwood. It all came back to Lockwood. The man had taken Leara from him before, all those years ago, when Garreth had been too involved in his own life to see that it would be empty without her. Lockwood hadn't ever given up; he'd been there waiting to step into the breach the moment there'd been a rift.

His anger burned into a white-hot flame. So, how could she have slept with Lockwood? If he hadn't gone by to pick her up early, would he have ever found out?

Garreth looked up at the street, trying to focus on the objects around him. He was glad now that Jenny had refused to come with him. He didn't know how he would have explained this to her. He didn't know if he could explain it to himself.

He pulled his keys from the ignition and got out of the car, unable to endure its confines. He had to breathe again.

Garreth walked swiftly, without a conscious destination, until he found himself in front of the gym where he usually worked out.

Garreth had tried to work off his consuming anger on the handball court as he'd trounced two consecutive opponents. Finally, he collapsed on a bench, panting, sweating, exhausted, but with the specter of Leara molding herself to Lockwood's body unexorcised and the desire to plant his fist into Lockwood's face stronger than when he'd started playing.

Without considering how foolish it was, he jumped up from the bench and slammed out of the gym, not even stopping to shower.

Fifteen minutes later, Garreth parked in front of Quint's dealership. Looking like an avenging god, his face dark, his features tense, he entered Quint's office. Finding the man alone, Garreth locked the door.

"Leave her alone," he said quietly, without preamble. He advanced menacingly. "If I ever see you near her—"

Quint, who'd been seated behind his desk, stood,

meeting Garreth's anger with a satisfied smile. "Did the lady tell you *she* called *me*, Conroe?"

Garreth stopped. The words bore into him, making his stomach knot in denial. His hand clenched into a fist. "She didn't!"

"Yes. She called. Said she *needed* to see me. She told me where to find her. I guess, after making love to you again—"

Quint ground to a halt. His face, losing its easy smirk, suddenly twisted with emotion. Thrusting his hands deep in his pockets, he turned to the window and looked out at the rows of cars. "After making love to you, I guess she just had to compare and see if she could find the same chemistry with me still."

"No!" Garreth started forward again, his anger sending imperative messages to his fingers to squeeze Quint's throat, to shut off the lies. Quint's next words stopped him cold, robbing him of the enervating anger and leaving him empty.

"Leara *was* married to me for eight years, Conroe. Do you really believe it could have lasted so long if there was nothing there? Anyway, our problems were never in the sack. Still aren't."

What had he expected? Garreth thought now, still possessed by that feeling of emptiness. He had dared to dream of a future with Leara again. Again his dreams had crashed and burned, leaving him surrounded by cold and ash.

The difference was that this time he wasn't foolish enough to think it was his fault. Leara wanted Lockwood.

Obviously, she always had.

Leara sipped her coffee, staring out the kitchen door at the sadly neglected backyard. M.J. had had the grass mown weekly, but weeds grew in the fence and flower beds and Gram's clothesline sagged, the posts rusting and leaning.

A brief smile touched her lips as she remembered how Gram had always insisted on hanging the bed sheets and table linen, even after her father had bought Gram an electric dryer. Leara remembered the wonderful smell of the sunshine-warmed fabric as she pressed her face into those sheets as she took them from the clothesline.

She had half thought she'd take the house off the market if she'd moved back to Columbus—revive the flower beds and put up another clothesline . . . if things had worked out . . .

Leara swallowed down the lump that rose in her throat and turned away from the door. The picnic hamper she'd packed Saturday morning with such anticipation of a day spent with Garreth still sat on the counter. When hours had passed and Garreth still hadn't come for her or called, she'd unpacked it, telling herself that he'd been called away suddenly on business. After all, hadn't he told her that his firm had projects going in all four corners of the country?

She'd determinedly shushed that niggling voice that reminded her he could have sent a message. Taped a note on her door on his way out of town. Sent up a smoke signal—something.

She'd ignored the sinking feeling she'd had inside as she'd trudged down to the convenience store on the corner and tried to call him, leaving messages on his machine. That voice inside had grown louder and more taunting when she had called again and found the machine turned off.

Leara sat the empty Styrofoam cup in the sink and paced the kitchen, her steps ringing hollowly on the old linoleum and echoing in the empty house. Garreth hadn't been called out of town on business—she felt it.

He was still here. Then why? Why was he doing this? Standing her up, ignoring her calls—why?

Oh, Garreth! Has this all been to set me up? Have you just been setting me up, and now you're paying me back for what I did years ago?

She'd gotten Teresa's number out of the phone book and called several times before catching her at home. Instead of the warm, friendly person she'd helped with Jenny's party, Teresa had been decidedly cool to her. To each of her questions about Garreth, Teresa had offered no answers, only a vague "I wouldn't know."

"Why?" Leara spoke the one syllable aloud. It filled the empty house.

Was Garreth paying her back? No, she couldn't believe that—his feelings had been too real. She read them in his eyes!

If not that, what? Could he have driven up while Quint was kissing her? Leara hugged herself tightly and shook her head in misery as she imagined that having happened. She imagined his pain at what he might have thought he was seeing—her in a robe and Quint kissing her good-bye after staying the night!

My God, if Garreth had seen Quint and thought that, he'd be so hurt! He'd see it happening again, just like ten years ago when she'd married Quint!

And Garreth might never trust her again. He'd been hurt too much by her desertion in the past. Now, how would she ever convince him that she hadn't been in Quint's arms willingly!

Quint! You must have seen Garreth coming—you rat!

Leara suddenly became aware of voices on the front porch. *Not now,* she thought, identifying one as M.J.'s.

Resignedly, she went to see.

"Hi! I was surprised when I saw your car here, Leara. I didn't expect to find you in town on a big Monday morning. That might explain why Coach didn't

make the Little League game yesterday afternoon.''
Marijo's black eyes sparkled.

Leara managed a wan smile. The last thing Leara
wanted right now was to explain anything to Marijo—
how could she? All she had was her own suppositions.
She didn't really know what was happening.

Marijo introduced Leara to a couple she'd brought to
view Gram's house, then immediately went into her
professional persona as she showed the couple through
the house. Leara faded into the background, thankful
M.J. was too preoccupied to notice that something was
wrong. Leara didn't feel like sharing her problems and
having M.J. ask all the questions she'd just asked herself without finding answers. She did smile as she
trailed after the trio as M.J. stopped at her old bedroom
and expounded on what a nice nursery it would make.
Then the smile grew watery as Leara saw the young
woman place her hand on her obviously pregnant stomach and share a special glance with her husband.

Garreth, Jenny, and their future children—she'd been
so close to having every dream come true!

Marijo left the couple in the kitchen. They were talking about how they could redecorate and modernize it,
and M.J. winked at Leara. "It's the third time I've
shown it to them, *niña*. I think it's as good as sold!"

Sold? Leara's stomach clenched as she looked around.
She blinked back tears as she realized she'd soon lose
this last connection with her past—with her father. And
Garreth.

"Lea? Is something wrong?"

"Just sentimental," she mumbled. "This was home."
But she'd left so much unfinished between her father
and herself. Though she'd tried time and time again
to contact him through the years—at Christmastime, at
Easter, or on his birthday—he'd erected a wall against
her and wouldn't let her in; hung up when he'd recog-

nized her voice; returned her letters unopened. He'd probably left her this house only because there was no other relative he could have left it to.

First her father had shut her out. Now Garreth— funny, she'd never seen that in some ways they were alike.

It was too late to make peace with her father. She'd be damned if she was going to let Garreth shut her out, too!

"Lock up?" Leara tossed over her shoulder as she headed for the door, escaping before the storm of tears she'd been holding inside could break.

"It seems that after Albert's near miss last month, this proposal from your partners is aimed expressly at avoiding the crowding above O'Hare. It *is* the country's busiest airport . . . Garreth? Are you in there?"

When she received no answer, Teresa sighed and gave up trying to discuss a proposal from the other partners in the firm to move their main office from Chicago to Columbus.

"Garreth, your body's here, but not your mind!"

"I know. Sorry." He rocked back in his desk chair and smiled ruefully. "I guess you could go on home. Maybe go ahead with that presentation we talked about for the Calgary project. I left some pencil sketches in the folder. You could use them to create the watercolor paintings."

"Okay." The blonde got up from her seat on the edge of the desk, plucked the folder in question off the credenza, and exited, leaving Garreth alone with his thoughts.

As the sound of Teresa's car died away, the ticking of the grandfather clock coming from the den began to seem excessively loud, reminding him that he was alone except for the maid. This was Jenny's fourth day at nursery school. She had started last Wednesday. Strange, he'd never noticed how empty the house seemed without the faint sounds of Jenny playing. Chelsea had helped him place her in Amelia's new nursery school for half a day and his child was blooming, always bursting with things to tell him about her day when she came through the door. Leara had certainly been right. . . .

Suddenly, violently, Garreth brought his fist crashing down on his desk.

The throbbing that radiated from it afterward was powerful. He was thinking what a damned fool he'd feel like if he'd broken a bone in it when he heard a car stop in the drive and wondered what Teresa could have forgotten.

The front door slammed, and he heard the maid's raised voice. There was the sharp sound of footsteps, and the office door flew open to bang against the wall.

SEVENTEEN

Leara strode into the room, her eyes flashing fire.

Lois trailed behind her. "I'm sorry, Mr. Conroe, I tried to tell her you—"

Garreth rose. "It's all right, Lois. Please close the door as you leave."

"What are you doing here?" he demanded when the maid left.

"I came for answers. You disappeared from my life three days ago and I want an explanation—"

"An explanation? *You* want an explanation! I should be the one demanding an explanation from you! What the hell *are* you doing here? You should be with your loving husband right now!"

"You saw Quint kissing me." Her words were flat. It was as she'd thought: he had seen her in Quint's arms, and he had assumed that she wanted to be there. Was there any way she could explain? Any explantion that he would accept? "You thought we had . . . been together."

"I saw you clutching at him like you never wanted to let go!"

"So you assumed the worst. You walked out of my life and never even gave me a chance to defend myself. And you accused *me* of running away all those years ago! At least I offered *you* a chance to make things right. You never even considered the possibility that things weren't as they seemed."

"The hell I didn't! I confronted Lockwood. He told me everything I needed to know. He told me *you* had called *him*, that you invited him over and went to bed with him, that it was *your* idea!"

Leara walked to the drawing board in the corner near the window, looking at the precise, clean lines of the sketch on it. She could hear Garreth's agitated breathing behind her. "Everything is supposed to fit, isn't it, Garreth? This master plan of yours for your life, with all the precise little pieces in their precise little places. And I was part of that plan, ten years ago. And part of the new one, now."

She turned to face him. His face was dark with anger, his hands clenched at his sides. But something else looked out of his eyes. A pain so deep that it transcended anything she had ever seen. A part of her heart went out to him, but she was angry, too.

"Well, life doesn't always follow our carefuly drawn up blueprints. Other people don't always follow our plans. Like Jenny. Like Quint. He used your jealousy against you. And against me. He tricked me—he had to have seen you coming. I wanted no part of him, or of that kiss. I had to yank his hair to get him to let me go." She saw her words reach him, but his doubts still had control. "I told him to get the hell of my life and stay out of it!

"Quint is a part of who I am. If it wasn't for my years as Quint's wife, I wouldn't *be* who I am. I learned that I *was* strong and could handle things—I had to! I soon learned that I couldn't lean on Quint and count on him to solve my problems the way I'd always counted on you! And I learned, after the divorce, that I could get along completely on my own; that I didn't have to be an extension of a man. That's all part of the package.

"I don't love Quint! I felt sorry for him, and guilty that I used him, so I tried to be his friend. He just used that to play his little games, so I've quit trying. And, yes. I did call him and tell him to come over. The arsonist had tried to torch another center, and the man fit Quint's description. I had to ask him . . . well. Becky told me when I talked to her yesterday that the police had arrested the man—someone who had applied for a job with us but failed our psych test."

Garreth reached for her, his mind trying to deal with what she had said while his emotions wavered between anger and relief. He gently touched her shoulder. "Leara—"

"Don't!" The one word cut like a knife's edge as she brushed his hand off. "Don't touch me again!" She retreated a few steps away.

"You asked me a long time ago to trust you, Garreth. But you've never trusted me! I want someone to share my life with, and I thought that someone was you. But there can be no future for us without trust! The past is gone, Garreth! And *I'm* tired of reliving it!"

"Leara, I—"

"No! Don't talk. I'm too angry to listen to you!" She turned away, grabbing her purse and heading for the door.

"Leara, don't run away again!" He took an uncertain step, not sure if he should go after her or stay where he was.

She paused. "I'm not running away. I'm not the old

Leara. I have to get out of here. Go someplace where I can think.'' She was out the door and gone.

He stood very still, suddenly aware that he had lost his only chance at happiness.

Garreth sat at his desk, staring at the drawings spread on it. He had done these days ago.

The sketches of the large Victorian house Leara had fallen in love with showed it with a fenced yard. Behind the house, a carriage house was depicted, its shutters thrown wide but with glass in the openings. The sketches of the interior showed several rooms, each with a different purpose. The carriage house was to have been a day care center, fully conforming to state regulations. It was to have been Leara's.

The downstairs of the main house was divided into classrooms for Leara's adult learning center. The upstairs would have been a living area. The house was so huge that there was plenty of room on the upper floors for them to live: a room for Jenny, one for him and Leara, one for the children still in the future. Kitchen, dining room and den, playroom and office all fit into the two upper floors.

He had been willing to share Leara's dream, to make it his, just a few days ago. He had let the past destroy it all.

He began putting the drawings into a portfolio.

''Daddy?'' Jenny's tentative voice reached out to him from the doorway. Seeing Garreth at his desk, she skipped over to him. ''Daddy, I was a teapot today! Miss Janet had me stand in the circle and all the other kids sang a . . .'' Her voice trailed off. She stood before him, her little face puzzled.

''Daddy, why are you sad?''

''Sometimes people feel sad,'' he told her, reaching way down and dredging up a smile.

The child stood silent for a moment, thoughtful.

"I heard Lois telling Amelia's mommy that Leara was here but left mad. You miss Leara, huh, Daddy?"

"Yes, pumpkin, I do."

Garreth was startled as Jenny suddenly burst into tears.

"Why does Leara want me to go away?"

"Jenny!" Garreth was on his feet and had Jenny in his arms in a second. He carried her to the sofa that stretched along one wall. He lifted her chin with one finger, making her look at him.

"What do you mean, Jenny? Leara doesn't want you to go away."

"But Aunt Tee Dee said that she and my mommy had to live at school when they were little. And when I asked Mrs. Teagle if I'd have to live at a boarding when I went to nursie school, she said yes 'cause Leara told her she didn't want me around."

"Leara would never send you away! And I thought that you *liked* going to nursery school every morning." Garreth was struggling to understand what had his daughter so upset.

Jenny's eyes grew wide. "I go to day care!"

"Jenny, some people call it nursery school, some people call it day care. But it's what Leara wanted for you. She thought you'd be happier around other children every day."

"I didn't know that nurse-er-ry school was that place I go play and have fun." She rubbed her nose on the back of her hand.

Garreth gave her a tissue from the box on the desk, suddenly aware of what Jenny's problem had been. He wished Teagle were still around so that he could make her face what she had done to his daughter—out of some kind of spite.

But, right now, the most important thing was to set Jenny straight.

"Leara always wanted you to be happy, Jenny. If she and I got married, we'd both want you right here with us." He cuddled his daughter to him, wishing he hadn't been so blind about a lot of things. "Leara loves you, sweetie. She would never send you away. She'd never do anything to hurt you."

Jenny's face turned up to him and he felt his heart catch. Her worried expression still hadn't cleared. "Doesn't Leara love *you* anymore, Daddy?"

Garreth heard an echo of his own words come back to him: *Leara loves you. She'd never do anything to hurt you.*

Yes, Leara loved him. He hadn't done anything to hurt her, except not trust in that love. And that was the biggest wrong he could have done. He'd been telling himself that she was different, that she wasn't the girl of ten years ago, but he had never really believed it, until today. In his mind, he had still expected her to betray him.

What an idiot he was! Jenny had asked him the question that he had been asking himself ever since Leara had come back into his life. And he had been too caught up in the past to realize that he had what he had always wanted—Leara. And that this Leara, this strong independent woman, would never do anything to hurt him.

"C'mon, Jenny. We have to go find somebody."

Leara sat cross-legged on a blanket of cottonwood leaves on the bank of Tarzan's Lake, idly demolishing a dandelion flower. "Why are men so pigheaded?" she questioned the woman with curling coppery hair who stared back at her from the water. The woman looked blank—obviously she hadn't a clue. "Doesn't he know how much I love him? Doesn't he understand that I've loved him for all these years—that if I had wanted Quint, or even someone else, I'd have them?"

No, because she hadn't told him. She'd been waiting for him to say that he loved her first.

Who was pigheaded? asked the woman in the lake.

Yeah. Well. Leara drew in a deep breath, sampling the earthy scents of leaf mold and mud, and consciously willed herself to relax, trying to dispel her lingering anger at Garreth for not believing in her.

Would he ever be able to trust her completely? Would he always let the specter of the past come between them?

And, if he couldn't place his complete trust in her, what would she do?

"I'm moving back, even if it doesn't work out with Garreth. I'm coming home," she said aloud. The woman in the water nodded and smiled, and Leara felt more of the tension drain from her, experiencing a strange sense of release at having finally made the decision she'd been moving toward for the past several weeks.

It had been nice working with Becky. They had both benefited. But Leara knew a yearning to solo—create her own center, staff it, and run it on her own. Besides, with Theo as Becky's new partner, she wouldn't be leaving Becky in a crunch.

Funny how all the years she'd lived in Gary, she'd always felt it was temporary. Here, Columbus, was the place she'd always thought of as home.

And she'd never thought of Columbus without thinking of Garreth.

Yes, she was coming home. To Columbus. And to Garreth, if he could accept her as she was. If not . . .

Leara's mind shied away from that possibility. The thought was just too painful to face.

Leara tugged at her collar. The day was hot and she felt sticky. It was kind of silly to sit here in the heat. Anyway, she'd found the answers she'd come here to find; made her decision.

She rose to leave. As she brushed off her jeans, Leara became aware of the sound of a car engine.

Garreth! She felt a surge of joy. It quickly evaporated as she thought of another possibility: it could be some stranger!

She listened intently as a car door shut. When she heard someone coming down the path, Leara edged back into the concealing foliage until she could see who approached. If it was a stranger, she could circle through the woods and get back to her car.

"Garreth!" Leara came out of her hiding place and waved as he appeared about fifty yards away.

"Look, Daddy!" Jenny pointed when she saw Leara. "Leara! Leara!" Jenny squirmed to get down. "I like nursery school! I thought I wouldn't 'cause I'd have to *live* there, but I *don't* and I like it! Amelia goes with me and my new friend Rosie is there—Daddy, put me down, please?"

"No, there are stickers and poison ivy and I can walk faster than you can."

"But you don't always take me where I want to go."

Leara felt tears prick her eyes at the sight of Jenny's eager smile. The child's rejection had hurt her a lot more than she had let Garreth know.

The sight of Garreth's smile made her tears flow. As she and Garreth closed the last few yards separating them, Leara held out her arms. "Would you like to come to me, Jenny?"

Jenny leaned so far out of her father's arms that if Leara hadn't caught her, she would have fallen. Leara's heart sang at the child's show of complete trust.

"I missed you!" Leara said, giving Jenny a hug.

"I missed you." Jenny pushed back in her arms and studied her solemnly. "Do you want to hug Daddy, too? He's been sad."

"Yes," Leara smiled through her tears. "I want to hug him very much. I've been wanting to hug him for days and days."

"Leara, I was stupid. I should have known that you couldn't do that to me. One thing you *never* did was lie. You were always straight with me."

Leara's heart was pounding with her joy, but still she waited. He had things to tell her, things she wanted to hear.

"I didn't come to you because I was afraid of the answers I might get. I didn't want to lose you again. I couldn't bear to lose you again." His arms were circling her and Jenny, but the look in his eyes was for her alone. His voice was soft when he continued, "I love you, Leara. I always have." He leaned toward her, about to place a kiss on her mouth.

"Daddy!" Jenny was tugging on his shirt. "Daddy!"

"What is it, Jenny?" Garreth pulled back to look at his daughter.

"Aren't you *ever* going to ask Leara to marry us?"

Garreth grinned, but his eyes were full of tenderness as he looked at Leara. "Well, Lea?"

"You two just tell me when. I'll be there." As Garreth's kiss sealed the promise, Leara placed a cloudy, heart-shaped stone in his hand.

SHARE THE FUN . . .
SHARE YOUR NEW-FOUND TREASURE!!

You don't want to let your new books out of your sight?
That's okay. Your friends can get their own. Order below.

No. 86 MAVERICK'S LADY by Linda Jenkins
Bentley considered herself worldly but she was not prepared for Reid.

No. 87 ALL THROUGH THE HOUSE by Janice Bartlett
Abigail is just doing her job but Nate blocks her every move.

No. 88 MORE THAN A MEMORY by Lois Faye Dyer
Cole and Melanie both still burn from the heat of that long ago summer.

No. 89 JUST ONE KISS by Carole Dean
Michael is Nikki's guardian angel and too handsome for his own good.

No. 90 HOLD BACK THE NIGHT by Sandra Steffen
Shane is a man with a mission and ready for anything . . . except Starr.

No. 91 FIRST MATE by Susan Macias
It only takes a minute for Mac to see that Amy isn't so little anymore.

No. 92 TO LOVE AGAIN by Dana Lynn Hites
Cord thought just one kiss would be enough. But Honey proved him wrong!

No. 93 NO LIMIT TO LOVE by Kate Freiman
Lisa was called the ''little boss'' and Bruiser didn't like it one bit!

Meteor Publishing Corporation
Dept. 1292, P. O. Box 41820, Philadelphia, PA 19101-9828

Please send the books I've indicated below. Check or money order (U.S. Dollars only)—no cash, stamps or C.O.D.s (PA residents, add 6% sales tax). I am enclosing $2.95 plus 75¢ handling fee for *each* book ordered.

Total Amount Enclosed: $_____.

____ No. 42	____ No. 76	____ No. 82	____ No. 88
____ No. 118	____ No. 77	____ No. 83	____ No. 89
____ No. 72	____ No. 78	____ No. 84	____ No. 90
____ No. 73	____ No. 79	____ No. 85	____ No. 91
____ No. 74	____ No. 80	____ No. 86	____ No. 92
____ No. 75	____ No. 81	____ No. 87	____ No. 93

Please Print:
Name _____
Address _____ Apt. No. _____
City/State _____ Zip _____

Allow four to six weeks for delivery. Quantities limited.